Linsey Abrams

Our History in New York

Global City Press, New York

ISBN 0-9641292-0-5

NOVELS BY LINSEY ABRAMS:
Charting by the Stars
Double Vision

The author wishes to gratefully acknowledge grants to work on this novel from the New York Foundation for the Arts and the New York State Council on the Arts, the latter while being Writer-in-Residence at the Harvey Milk School. She also wants to thank the editors at *Christopher Street*, Eve Ensler who edits *Central Park*, and David Milofsky, the editor of *The Colorado Review*, for publishing, respectively, "True Love" (Chapter Eight), "Higher Powers" (Chapter Four) and "Gay Pride" (Chapter Six) in slightly altered form.

Our History in New York

A Novel

For Adria Schwartz, Charlotte Sheedy,
Ann Eugenia Volkes & William Wilson,
without whose help, each in a different way,
I would never have written this book,
and in memory of John Braswell, Ty French,
Gregory Kolovakos & James Yassky.

"Identity is recognition, you know who you are because you and others remember...."

—Gertrude Stein

Chapters

Our History in New York

Arcturian Consciousness

It was a Saturday evening in September that Monica called to tell me Rodger was dying. It made sense, once she said it. Why else would a fifty-year-old stage director leave New York for Niles, Ohio? A few months earlier, Rodger had resigned his advisory role at the Off Off Broadway company he'd been associated with for twenty years.

"I guess a part of me knew he had AIDS," I told her, after she'd gotten out the words. "But I kept thinking that if he really did, somebody would have told me. I had this crazy hope he'd gone home to get sober," I admitted.

I thought back to a decade earlier, during the time when Rodger and I had been so close. I don't know how we kept up that pace, myself assistant-managing the company as well as working on Rodger's productions, and him in class all day, then at the theater evenings. He must have directed a hundred plays, and written dozens, before the alcohol soured even his genius.

"He made me promise to keep it a secret," Monica said. "Only now there's going to be a reception in New York...at the theater. He wants to see everybody before he dies," she added. "I just got off the phone with him."

"Was it awful, Monica?"

"No more so than usual."

"Was he drunk?" I asked.

"Was he drunk," she repeated my words. "They're staying at the Gramercy Park, while Lou"—Lou was Rodger's mother—"is trying to sell his apartment and settle his affairs...But he's getting more and more out of hand, which is why they're pushing the reception up to Sunday."

"You don't mean tomorrow," I said.

"Unfortunately, I do," she answered. "It was supposed to be next week, but Lou can't stand to prolong the trip. Rodger stays on the phone all night in their hotel suite, calling all the people he ever knew to tell them what he thinks of them. In Ohio, it's easier, because he has his own floor of the house."

I wasn't surprised Rodger hadn't phoned me. It had been years since I'd gotten those middle-of-the-night calls that I stopped responding to after I stopped drinking. But you don't have that kind of intense friendship with someone then just quit loving them. I'd known Rodger since Monica and I had been his theater students in college.

"I've got to get off now, Chloe," Monica said. "I'm at work, and I've still got thirty-eight people to call." She laughed, the way she always used to when Rodger had asked for the impossible, which was his specialty.

Suddenly, the sound took me back to that life from long ago, when we did everything and went everywhere with a whole cast and crew of people. I remembered the exact feeling of being in production...the way, as a child, you take such pleasure in putting life in the service of fantasy. I thought of a little girl I knew, who, for a year, addressed her parents as "Queen" and "King", and asked to be called "Beauty." The three of them wore paper crowns when by themselves in the house.

"At this rate, you'll be on the phone all night," I told Monica. "Actually, I've got to go, too...Helen and I are meeting some people." After we hung up, for a moment it seemed shameful to go on living.

*

We were meeting Rosalie and Alexandra in the East Village, not far from Helen's apartment. I took a cab so I wouldn't be late. But by the time I got to the restaurant, the others were already there. Helen beckoned, from a table near the window, as I made my way past the crowded bar into the dining room. The two doctors waved.

I told everyone about Rodger. In answer, Alex reported her own phone call from a friend, saying he had bad news...about their mutual friend Hogan, who owns Hogan's Heroes, a deli on Columbus Avenue. Alex said it was insane, but she'd actually been relieved to hear that at thirty-eight, he'd suffered a massive heart attack, from which it was possible he just might recover. Rosalie mentioned another man they were close to, also in his thirties, who had thrown his second annual last birthday party in August. He wore a Roman toga, two condoms as earrings, and the very next morning began a course of AZT. As planned, each of the twenty guests had arrived also in a toga and with a vase of cut flowers, until every surface in the tiny, L-shaped studio was crowded with glorious growth.

"Why the togas?" I asked.

"It was a 'Decline and Fall of the Empire' party," replied Rosalie. The four of us nodded.

"We went to the party as prostitutes, the only women who got out of the house in ancient Rome," Alex said. But it was impossible to imagine those two doctors passing themselves off as whores. I pictured the skeletal, crack-addicted women who flag down cars on Twelfth Street, their faces painted garish as clowns, their spirits so disembodied they move the way you'd imagine mannequins come to life, jerky and without feeling tone.

As a waitress approached with menus, I looked around the restaurant, new that month and on East Fourth Street, once the mecca of Off Off Broadway. Rodger and I had worked together just up the block.

"Is the world really more terrible now than it's ever been, or does it just seem that way?" I asked, after we'd ordered.

"Sometimes I think that in the information age we're just more aware of everything that goes on. Both the good *and* the bad," said Rosalie. "I guess you have to weigh modern dentistry, antibiotics, psychoanalysis, the theory of evolution, and birth control against the rest of it." Working on a locked psychiatric ward, Rosalie tends to take the long view.

"You're talking about television," Helen responded. "*Television* is what's given us that awareness..."

Her comment made me think about a night, a few years before, when we'd met after work...myself exhilarated from a graduate class I'd taught on how Beckett's *Endgame* and Aeschylus's *Oresteia* employ similar rhetorical modes in the portrayal of domestic tragedy...and Helen speechless from having screened four videocassettes of a man who had just massacred his estranged wife and children and was threatening to jump from a project roof. In the fifth tape, he did. It's the sounds, Helen says, that stay with you afterwards.

"Marshall MacLuhan," Alexandra uttered the name of the Canadian media guru whose theories we had once held in such reverence. "That was one of MacLuhan's points. 'The medium is the message.'"

"He predicted everything," agreed Helen, who sits all day in an edit room with two TVs, one playing the tape she's editing and the other on network programming or an in-house feed that plays movies and specials. It used to play pornography, until 1978, when the two dozen or so women the network had hired by then filed a class action suit.

At the time, the only person more popular than MacLuhan was Buckminster Fuller, whose vision of the future was utopian, thus more in keeping with the spirit of hope we had in that era, in spite of everything. Several of my friends dropped out of college to build geodesic domes, in New Hampshire, where they intended to live forever. It was pleasant to think of ourselves as forms of energy, in our twenties, when we had more of it.

"I was watching a talk show on cable, the other day," Helen

continued, after our waitress had set down the plates. "One of the guests was a man who was quite knowledgeable about the world's religions...he spoke about early Christianity, Judaism, Buddhism, and even quoted the Koran. When the host asked him if he was a Christian, he said that no, he was an *estericist*."

"That sounds sensible," Rosalie commented.

"Yes, but what he said next, wasn't," Helen replied. "He said that God had entered the body of a Pakistani man in London in 1977, and that that's who is going to save the world."

"Well, I'm glad *someone's* volunteered," said Alex.

"Actually, there are other candidates," Helen informed her. "The second guest was an independently wealthy person who said he was a philanthropist. But it turned out that the people he gives money to, as well as the man himself, are all from another planet...or rather their consciousness is. The planet's called *Arcturus*."

"How did the host react to this?" asked Rosalie.

"He didn't seem to have a problem, until the other Arcturians identified themselves in the audience. There were about a dozen of them, all dressed in Brooks Brothers suits and what looked like Albert Nippon dresses." Helen was in fashion design, before TV, and has an eye for clothes. "They were tall, perfectly groomed, and every one of them was blond," she said. "They looked like Nazis. Then it came out that they had all gone to Yale, Harvard, Stanford, or Princeton, which is when the host went off the deep end. He became irate."

"I can see that," I said. "It's one thing for them to say they're from another planet, but when you find out they've all achieved more success at being people than the rest of us, it's upsetting."

"Who was the host?" Alexandra wanted to know.

"Bob Stewart...from Earth," Helen said.

"Bob Stewart probably didn't go to college," mused Rosalie. It occurred to me that once upon a time, a psychiatrist's remarks must have stood out, while they don't anymore, because now *everybody* sounds like a psychiatrist.

"Well, the philanthropist Arcturian's prediction was that in June the world's going all to hell," Helen continued.

"This June?" Alex, whose immunological research takes months to show results, looked genuinely concerned.

"Yes. First, the stock market's going to crash again, *really* this time he said, then there are going to be tidal waves and earthquakes. After that, the Arcturians, and not the Pakistani who was entered by God in London, are going to take over." Helen smiled, then continued, "They're going to ban all nuclear energy and future toxic waste, return government to localities, and stop discrimination because of age, race, national origin, sexual orientation, or gender by the end of the century. They're also going to stop warfare and use the worldwide defense budget for AIDS and breast cancer research, among other things." Our table applauded.

"That's exactly right," said Alexandra. She paused, before adding, "I wonder if I'm an alien, too. I did attend Stanford for a fellowship year."

"You're the wrong ethnic group," Rosalie reminded her. "They don't give Arcturian consciousness to Greeks."

Alex shrugged.

"Do they really think they're from another planet, all those people who went to Harvard and Yale?" I asked. "I thought an education was supposed to *protect* you from irrational belief."

"You wish it, Professor," said Helen, who never went to college herself. "But, the fact is, none of them believes it...they just pretend to, because of the money the philanthropist gives them."

"They believe in Arcturus because they've been driven to it," I said. "The fact is, they've placed their hope elsewhere...because they're afraid it's beyond *human* capability to solve the terrible problems we have today."

"Well, if the rest of the studio audience that afternoon was an indication of human capability, then they're right, we're in trouble," Helen answered. "People kept shouting out 'Heresy!' or quoting the Bible. One woman swore she'd never let her son attend an Ivy League college and got a standing ovation. Someone even suggested a boycott of Pakistan. These people were crazier than the Arcturians, and no one even noticed."

"I'll say," said Rosalie, who ought to know.

Later, the four of us kissed good-night in front of the restaurant. Alex and Rosalie went west on Fourth Street, while Helen and I walked to Second Avenue. As we headed uptown, winos, punks, and people more like us took turns dominating the sidewalk. Eighth Street had the highest concentration of humanity: People doing drug deals and playing pinball...making phone calls. Junkies selling each other useless items: three-month-old *Esquires*, boots the wrong size.

In front of the plate glass of a Polish coffee shop stood a bunch of teenagers, skull-and-crossbones stamped in denim where before people had sewn peace symbols. The hair of those who hadn't shaved their heads bald was crested like parrots and dyed the same brilliant colors.

"It's a full moon," Helen said, glancing overhead.

"It's always a full moon in this neighborhood," I replied.

That celestial body looked smaller in the sky than it sometimes does, but round and with a glow that made sunshine seem plain.

"Dan used to hate working in the ER on Saturday nights, holidays and the full moon," Helen added. "There's more violence...gunshot wounds, beatings. Accidents. More suicides..." She was referring to an old boyfriend, one of her two important ones, someone she might have married if they'd been that age five years earlier. But by the seventies people just lived together.

"I remember the only time I saw him being a doctor," Helen said as we crossed Eighth Street and passed the building where they'd torn out the two-dollar movie theater to make some kind of mall you'd never have expected to see in the land of headshops and vintage clothing. "Tonight, being with Rosalie and Alex, made me think of it.

"It was when Dan was just a fourth-year medical student and working in the ER at St. Vincent's. The residents gave them all this responsibility when they didn't know anything, because the residents didn't want to come in. It was the Fourth of July, and I was there because we were planning to go out for Chinese food on his dinner break, at six," Helen added. That's the kind of detail she remembers, the time of somebody else's dinner break, fifteen years ago. "Just that week, he'd gotten an offer from a friend of his uncle to join a plastic surgery practice in Connecticut, and he wanted to discuss it. We were both so busy then, we never had time to talk. We hardly saw each other. I was working on Seventh Avenue and he was always in class or at the hospital. But the relationship wasn't in such good shape, either."

A reading was letting out as we passed St. Mark's Church. I recognized the diehard poetry crowd from the books and flyers in their hands, their necessary talk.

"But suddenly this drug OD was wheeled into the waiting room," Helen continued, "and the four of them on duty that night ran out to the girl, who lay slumped on the pallet. They fastened on her, shouting, 'What did you take? Tell us what you took...' But she was delirious...Those doctors sounded like insane drug dealers, shouting out their wares," Helen said. "*Acid, mescaline, STP, heroin, Quaaludes,speed*. Everybody looked up from books or injuries to listen with rapt attention."

The med students tried to shake her awake, even slapped her face, to shock her into answering. But the girl just writhed around, silent as some animal in pain, while they kept shouting, "What did you take?" Helen said it was upsetting to see four men treat a woman that way, even if it was in hopes of saving her. She was one of those twenty-year-olds with the kind of child body that attracts danger. You see pictures of those girls all the time in the newspaper, from when they were in high school and still alive.

"What *did* she take?" I asked.

"Opium. She ate it...an enormous amount," Helen replied. "Dan said it was crazy, after seeing the results of the autopsy. That girl was the first patient...the first person... Dan ever saw die. Well, he finally got off for dinner at 11:45," she continued. "I'd been there reading Kate Millet's *Sexual Politics* since six. We broke up because of that book... indirectly.

"So we went to this Chinese restaurant," Helen went on, "and before we even ordered they gave us a plate of fortune cookies, because our waiter got us mixed up with the next table, where they'd asked for the check. There were maybe eight of them who'd just been to an EST meeting...on the Fourth of July, mind you. All they talked about was pushing each other's buttons and how this one girl had to take responsibility for not finding a parking place near the restaurant."

Listening to Helen, I remembered how, after Vietnam, something shifted in this country...at least for people our age. Maybe it was because nobody believed you could change the world any more that they tried changing themselves, through EST seminars, rebirthing, yoga retreats. I knew a dozen people who followed Swami Satchidananda, some macrobiotics, a Sullivanian...looking to change their bodies or their minds. But the rest of us were offended, I think...having come of age during that terrible war...by how little people were valued for who they were already—without improvement, just by dint of being human.

"Well, we both went into the ladies' room to smoke a joint," Helen said, "to calm ourselves down. After the EST people left, we were the only ones there...it was a holiday so business was slow...Some people would think that's ironic, or immoral, after a drug OD, but the two events aren't even in the same category."

"Who knew that drugs would turn into *this*," I said, waving my hand up Second Avenue. "*Recreational* is a word of the past." Helen nodded.

"All Dan kept saying after we got back to the table," she went on, "was that he was either going to take the practice in Connecticut or quit medicine. Because, and this is the exact way he put it," Helen said, stopping in front of the paper stand on Eleventh Street, "because a doctor's job is not to cure anybody...basically the body heals itself or it doesn't... his job is to witness death." Helen sighed. "I argued with him all night. Literally," she said, taking out her wallet. "It was one of those twenty-four-hour Chinese restaurants...But by the time we went home to sleep, at 8:00 AM, I had him convinced not to give up."

Standing so tall, her hair a mass of dark unruly curls, and opinionated as she is, Helen must have scared the men she slept with then. Sometimes she scares me. We bought the *Times* and continued home.

"It's funny," she mused, "all these years later, after everything, Dan being in Papua, New Guinea, with his family and me here in New York with you."

Over the summer, he'd written that the medical procedures he performs most often now are amputations and "thoracotomies," which we found out means "removing arrows from the chest." Dan sent a photograph, taken by his wife, Emily, of three bush people on a bench, looking curiously at the camera, with him standing to the side, extending a swab to an infected foot. He looks as astounded by the circumstances as his patients, the one with the above-mentioned foot the size of a football, another with a back as mottled by skin disease as if it were tattooed, and the third a dwarfed woman with arms at the top of her shoulders like bird wings. Dan and Emily and their two little daughters, who in another photo posed barechested with longbows, intended to stay in Papua, New Guinea, another year before returning to Cleveland, where Dan has practiced in a public clinic since 1974, when he and Helen broke up.

In front of us I saw a bunch of red hats...the Guardian Angels on patrol. It was only since they'd volunteered their services, that summer, and been given a ground-level apartment on Thirteenth Street, that the couple of blocks around Helen's had started to get cleaned up. A lot of people thought they were some kind of paramilitary vigilante group, at first. But two weeks after they came, you could walk home at night without running into bands of boys, on their toes like prizefighters, high on testosterone and crack.

Their organization boarded up the abandoned building at the corner; local businesses donated nails, lumber, barbed wire, and tools. A dry goods merchant, relocated from Vienna, '39, fashioned a banner with their favorite slogan, "Crack is whack...life is fresh." They hung it from the second-floor fire escape of their headquarters, where the restaurants took turns delivering free meals: sushi rolls and blintzes, curries and Opera cake, mushu pork, falafels, nouvelle cuisine.

As the teenagers approached on the sidewalk, their stride was purposeful. Looking snappy in their berets, the young men and women saluted us as they passed. It seemed ironic, them coming here from their burnt-out neighborhoods in the South Bronx and Harlem to save East Thirteenth Street.

"And about those fortune cookies..." Helen said, as we walked up the steps of her building into the lobby. "I decided that since Dan was the one with the decision to make and I was just living my life, he would have one fortune and I'd have all the rest. His read, and I swear, 'You were put on this earth to help others.' Really," Helen said, pulling out her keys and opening the door.

"Did any of yours come true?" I asked her.

"Those that I remember," she replied. "One said I would find true love." Helen pointed at me. "Another said that my principles meant more to me than success or money. A third one said I would inspire other people to do their best. And a fourth one..." Here she paused to unlock the apartment door. "The fourth one said I would live a long and interesting life."

We looked at each other, before Helen turned the doorknob and pushed inside.

It was a big turnout, at six the next evening, on the stage proper where people had congregated for Rodger's reception. It had been so many years since I'd stage-managed there, or even attended productions, that I'd wondered if I would know anybody. But Marcel had been on the door, looking the same albeit paunchier and with thinning hair, and once inside I recognized a handful of famous and not-so-famous actors, the lighting designer Olivia deScenza, plus a few of the tech crew from my era.

Scattered throughout the crowd were kids I took to be Rodger's recent students. I also recognized some of his colleagues, men mostly, in corduroy jackets and thick-rimmed glasses, gathered at the refreshment table. As I made my way through the crowd, I exchanged greetings with several people I was glad to see.

"He's in Phebe's, and they can't talk him into coming over. He keeps saying he wants one more drink." Monica took me by the elbow and pulled me into the wings. "Arthur's gone over there," she added, referring to the theater's director, who for decades had loved Rodger's work, and Rodger, if the truth be known. But from the beginning he'd gotten in over his head in that relationship.

As we stepped back from embracing, I marveled at how beautiful Monica still was, though it would never be quite the same as when I first knew her and she gave off a sense of the world much bigger than herself, like a rose in full bloom. I don't remember what Monica said, at first, because she was one of those friends with whom conversation isn't the shared language. Her physicality dominated everything...the slight curl of her lip into a characteristically rueful smile, her slouch that had become exaggerated over the years, a kind of boniness about her shoulders that made people want to hold them. The single element of her appearance that had remained the same since girlhood was her eyes...a hazel color that reminded me of lilacs, unnatural in a human face.

"They sent a limo for the two of them up at the hotel. But Rodger just gave them the address up the street, then hopped out and began ordering stingers. I've been over there twice myself. Even Lou can't budge him."

When Rodger was on a binge, this was not untypical behavior, and as the years had passed, he was more usually on a binge than not. I always figured the alcohol was what would kill him.

"Is Emil going to be here?" I asked Monica.

"No," she answered.

Emil had been Rodger's lover for a decade, directing him in plays and underground movies in the sixties, before Rodger became a director himself. The two collaborated on what turned out to be the best work of each, though later Emil would become successful, by popular standards, working for Hollywood. Their relationship was dramatic and ended predictably, when Emil, quite a bit older than Rodger, began sleeping with even younger protégés. Rodger moved out of their apartment on 57th Street into the Y, where he lived for six months before being arrested on a morals charge.

"You've heard that Emil's sick, too?" Monica added.

"Yes," I told her. "Every time you get a phone call, you hear about someone else."

There was a commotion and we turned downstage, where out among the two-hundred-seat house you could see, at the back of the center aisle, a knot of people. I lost my breath, as I glimpsed in the melee the familiar movement of an arm, a quarter profile of a face that I both recognized, and didn't... But I was sure it was Rodger from that particular sense you have of your body in another's presence...different for each person you know, extraordinary as that fact is. I realized, as some old part of me leaped in my chest, how little time had changed my feelings for him.

People turned to look, stopping talking then starting again;

the silence had seemed oppressive, singling Rodger out in a way none of the rest of us would want to have been. But he was ready for our attention. Rodger emerged from those around him, to walk by himself toward the stage.

He looked ancient...like some puppet made of wood, in the way his cheeks were carved hollow...his limbs pendulous and thin as jointed sticks as he wobbled, his steps too wide... Pinocchio aged. A fierce concentration directed his navigation: he saw nothing but what was directly before his gaze. He was drunk in the way of people who start in the morning, so much alcohol in his system you wondered how he could stay upright.

With sudden clarity, I remembered a night, years before, when we were in production together at a theater on 42nd Street. Several new companies had just sprung up there... Playwrights Horizons, the Puerto Rican Voice, now defunct, and some others...opposite the highrises built to house actors. It was spring, during one of those not infrequent seasons when Rodger was on the outs with Arthur and would make deals to direct elsewhere.

A basement, our space got so clammy during rehearsals, with most of the lights out, that its temperature stayed a good ten degrees cooler than outside. We called it Siberia Rep. That night, a bunch of us were going upstairs to the warm air, when suddenly Rodger's legs collapsed. It was something like dreaming, the way he just picked himself up, dusted off his elbows, and without mentioning the fall, continued his stream of consciousness to the handful of young men left over after rehearsal. If he hadn't been so talented, his career would have been over because of the drinking. But people figured he was still worth the trouble then.

On the sidewalk, we met Moishe, who managed the row of buildings where our theater was housed. He was squat and balding, and though he wore expensively tailored suits, his body filled them out in the wrong places. He was the kind of man you couldn't imagine having a family, or any kind of life beyond 42nd Street, which up until recently had housed only porn theaters and massage parlors. We got to talking about how the neighborhood had changed, and it ended up him letting us in the back door of a strip joint he also managed up the street. I went out of curiosity.

You might wonder how it feels to be a woman, and a lesbian, in a room full of men waiting for somebody with the same anatomy as you to take off her clothes to canned music. The men just standing about...some with their arms draping each other's shoulders...others more private, paying attention to their fantasies. The loud talk among the former, the gum snapping, the male energy. The latter utterly still, like boys with a dragonfly on a finger. You could see Rodger's eyes roam to the crowd in front of us then to the stage. He'd been married, to a woman he said he'd loved, before beginning the affair with Emil. We were way in the back, under orders from Moishe, who thought it might upset "the girls," as he called them, to see me. It's funny what upsets people.

The woman who started the show wasn't pretty, with hair dyed red once too often, a face pocked as brocade, and she wasn't happy. Nor were any of the string of "girls" that came after her, old girls, their chests large but sagging, like sprung couches. I was prepared when a man strode up to the stage and started fondling a woman's breasts and even when, after that, two of them knocked shoulders to reach a hand between her legs. But what caught my attention, and startled me, was that the men talked to each other all through it, and never once looked into her face. She didn't smile; she didn't pretend to enjoy any of it. That's when I understood, she wasn't supposed to.

It's not the kind of thing I expected to see when I was twenty-five, though by that age I'd seen a lot of what I never expected to see. Men started to come forward, the women walking bowlegged to the edge of the raised stage. I saw a ten-dollar bill disappear between a woman's thighs, then another. Even at the time, I did not believe I was witnessing *desire*.

The gay club where we ended up was nearby in the 40s, flowers everywhere, beautiful blond boys in track suits tending bar, the dance floor filled with men, hundreds of them packed in body to body, and my only recall after a certain point...the way alcohol makes a tunnel of your mind, and you're always at the far end from the light...was taking the elevator up. Suddenly we were on the roof, the stars like a crown of jewels overhead, and someone with a Polaroid was taking photographs of a long line of men.

Rodger and I sat down on a water bed to watch them pose, singly and in couples. I'm sure that on other occasions that bed was used for sex. But even the hedonism of a homosexual male club seemed wholesome to me, after what we had witnessed at Moishe's. The men liked one another. They were equals.

As Rodger walked toward us, that September evening, the seats of the theater empty on either side, I thought of him as being flanked by the dead. I wondered how many of those who were photographed that night in 1975 had survived.

While he made his way forward, looking seventy years old when just a few months before he had been a lined but active fifty, I realized what quality it is that great stars have. Actually, I realized there are two kinds...the ones like Garbo or Deitrich who would spit on you and make you holy by their imperiousness...and the others, wholly innocent, which is what Rodger was, in spite of all he'd been through. When you see such people act, you want to call from the audience, Watch out! You want to take care of them.

By now my old friend had reached the stage. Monica held out her hand at the stairs. He was so light from what looked like a thirty-pound weight loss, or more, he almost floated up as she took his hand. He spoke to people, turning his head left and right as he made his way into the crowd. People he had known for years, he treated as if he were meeting for the first time. It was his students he was able to recognize, of everyone there. He embraced their youthful bodies.

Rodger shook hands, in turn, with each of his former colleagues, the men still gathered at the refreshment table, from which I myself hadn't strayed far. Their faces registered alarm, as bowing, he mocked their decorum.

"And you would *come* for me?" he posed a rhetorical question to the first of them. "And *you* would come for me?" he asked the next. Rodger repeated his question, until he had remarked to each one of them his amusement that they would show up to honor a dying man whose life they'd had no use for.

Suddenly, it was my turn. I wasn't sure whether he would choose to know me, if the step I had taken away from Rodger a long time ago could be retraced that night.

"I love you," I said, because suddenly everything else seemed irrelevant.

"I think I have always known that," Rodger answered, taking me in his arms. He continued to hold me, his posture seductive even now, an old habit. Then it was as if the kind of clay mask women wear at night cracked to reveal his true face. It's people's animation we think of as themselves. "What more can I say?" he asked, a question that was not rhetorical.

"I don't know," I said, shaking my head. Everything that had happened between the two of us, as well as his imminent death and the fact that I would live...was contained in the silence that followed.

"I love you, too, Chloe," he said a moment later, and I had always known that. But sometimes people say things for other reasons, to read them into the record of life in a different way.

When Rodger became a director, he was good at it because he was an actor, first, in his body, and now his body changed as once again he retreated into himself. He turned from me, very slowly letting go my waist then my hand until only the air between us was left charged.

I decided to remember Rodger the way he was that evening, emaciated and drunk as he came back to us from the Midwest. An apparition of a much older man than he would live to become. Because even in the absolute mania that prevailed in his behavior on and off throughout the reception, you could see something of the old Rodger, who after each fall would pick himself up and go on. Without fanfare or apology.

Ten minutes later, someone pulled down a screen for projections, and people started descending the trio of stairs on either side to take seats in the house. A girl and boy, in black leotards, lifted the table of wine and cheese then carried it offstage. I saw Lou, dressed in a Chanel suit and her hair coiffed like a large silver pearl, take Rodger's arm to direct him after them. Her healthy energy made her seem like his daughter. Now that's a mother's love, to become even the daughter to her son.

The stage lights went out. I followed on the heels of the crowd, finding a seat near the back on an aisle. The sound of a projector running insulated the tiny theater, before a strip illuminated the screen, bearing in black-and-white the title of Rodger's first film. It looked burned in.

Chimes is a cult classic from the sixties, shown every few years at Film Forum or the Museum of Modern Art. It was made soon after Rodger and Emil met. Shot in 16-millimeter, the movie looks, and rightly, like some kind of low-budget dream.

People were talking softly, making the air above the seats hum, until the familiar first closeup of Rodger filled the screen. There was scattered applause, then silence. Rodger was in his twenties at the time and not handsome really, but vitalized. So young-looking, his hair clipped close to his head, his gaze inviting while hard...he looked like a convict in love. Still, there was something in his repose that suggested immense feeling just below the surface.

Watching Rodger on screen made me think again about what makes a star, how in their person they represent the way the psyche binds opposites. I can't explain it except to add, he embodied that part of the other you make up yourself. The few times Rodger acted, as the years went on, at least the few times I saw him act, I always came away feeling *alive*. That's the gift real artists have. The rest are just businessmen in tights.

The film had been running about forty-five of its seventy minutes when I heard a cry behind me. Whoever it was made no attempt to stifle the sound. Soon I heard another person begin to sob, then a third. People in the theater are prone to being expressive; all the same I've never witnessed anything like what happened that night. For the next twenty-five minutes, people sat in the audience, weeping. It sounded like nothing I've heard before or since, at the end credits reaching the pitch of a siren, before I picked myself up and, tears streaming from my own eyes, made my way down the aisle to outside.

I crossed Second Avenue, sobbing. I can't say anybody noticed anything out of the ordinary. In this city you see people in all forms of extremity.

Two weeks later, I received the second phone call about Rodger. Rosalie called to report that he'd just been admitted to the psychiatric ward she supervises at St. Luke's.

"In New York? Rodger? I don't understand," I said, looking out my living room window at the sky.

"I thought you'd want to know," Rosalie replied. "Some friends of his persuaded him to commit himself, this afternoon. We'll be moving him to detox tonight. How he even got to New York in his condition is some kind of miracle. I'm surprised they let him board the airplane in Ohio."

"How much do you know?" I asked her. "Do you know why he's here?"

"I did the intake interview," Rosalie answered. "Some of it I heard from him, some from his friends, and then I called his mother."

"Lou..." I said.

"Lou hired some kind of attendant for him. But Rodger kept causing trouble. So she couldn't take it anymore and she left for Florida..."

"She has a house in Boca Raton," I told Rosalie.

"I guess that's where I called her then," she continued. "It seems he would leave the house, drunk, take her car and drive downtown, and go into all the stores and announce he had AIDS. Then he'd ask people to kiss him."

For a moment, neither of us spoke.

"At any rate, the last time he escaped the attendant, he somehow managed to get to the airport and board a plane for New York. This woman, Monica *something*, said she ran into him by coincidence in some bar in the East Village."

"I know her, too," I said. "We both worked with him for years."

"Your friend Rodger is in pretty rough shape," Rosalie concluded. "He's half dead from the alcohol, never mind the AIDS."

"How is he?" I asked. I don't know what answer I expected her to give me, beyond what she'd just said.

"He's sick and he's crazy," she replied. Rosalie paused. "Maybe he's not crazy, maybe he's just sad," she added carefully, which is her way. She's the most modest doctor I know.

"He's always been sad," I told her.

And I realized that I had loved Rodger all along because his life was ravaged—a condition more usually associated with women though a certain type of man is similarly not averse to wearing on the outside his despair at having lost the beloved's attention. Most men are exempt from such loss. They never risk intimacy at all, like the ones I remember with their paper money in their teeth, crowding the lighted stage.

"What's going to happen to him now?" I asked.

If only there was something you could see to do, something simple and right, like pulling an arrow from a chest.

"Well, I can't predict the future," Rosalie said. "But, if you're asking for my professional opinion, I'd say he's going to be in and out of hospitals, with both psychological and physical problems, until one time he isn't going to come out."

Impersonating Shirley MacLaine

Though Victor was one of the few people I knew who was always punctual if not early, that evening I got there first. I was meeting him in front of the Lesbian and Gay Community Center, where he'd been attending Act Up meetings every Monday. Actually, I'd been meaning to go with him, for months. But it was only after seeing Rodger again that I did.

I sat down on one of the benches outside the four-story building that had once been a vocational high school and watched people pass on the sidewalk. Clusters of men and women, some of them same-sex and some co-ed, stood talking nearby under a streetlight. Most were in their twenties and early thirties, displaying a kind of physicality that comes from the pleasure people take in their bodies at that age...part of which has to do with other people's pleasure in looking at them. The majority, I knew, would be heading inside a few minutes later for Act Up...or some other activity that was scheduled that night.

Victor arrived just then, in his standard fall attire...blue-jeans with a white shirt under a leather jacket. His sandy hair was pulled back into the usual ponytail, his beard a small cloud. Standing well over six feet, Victor stooped to kiss me.

"Have you been waiting long?" he asked. "Out here in the cold?" Victor always spoke as if life were some party at which he, for some unexplained reason, had been designated host... and things were not quite as nice as he'd have planned.

"Actually, I've been entertaining myself, contemplating youth and beauty," I said. Victor smiled, and glanced into the crowd on the sidewalk. Under the streetlight, the air made cones of their breath.

"Is it just my imagination, or do gay people look better than they used to?" he asked.

"As a group, I think we probably do look better," I said. "AIDS aside, it's not so stressful, now that it's possible to live at least part of your life out of the closet...and also people like themselves better now...which shows in their faces."

"That's the self-esteem issue...but there's also the clothing factor," said Victor, who worked as an articles editor at a fashion magazine. "Now that people can wear pretty much what they want, at least outside of corporations, they can find clothes that suit them better...that reflect more their sense of themselves, their image of their own sexuality...without having to go overboard the rest of the time. And just pragmatically, people have other ways, now, to let interested parties know that they're gay."

"Like telling them," I said. Victor and I both laughed, because we recalled the time, not so long ago really, when wild horses couldn't have dragged this information out of even the two of us.

"It was a constant parade in the Village," Victor remembered. "People would take to the streets on weekends...all the men wearing high leather or glow-in-the-dark caftans...and the women in that butch hair and the army/navy outfits."

"It was primitive," I said, "like birds. But in a way, I miss it, how people used to look. Now anybody who dresses outlandishly is nine times out of ten a schizophrenic...except for that man who impersonates Santa Claus and the one who always wears a Shakespearean tunic and tights...you know, with the Vandyke beard." Victor nodded.

"The transvestites were the true founders of gay liberation," he commented. "For years, even centuries, they were the only people out of the closet."

"Those people were very brave," I said.

"Not to mention, exhibitionists," Victor added.

The lobby was crowded, with people at the reception desk, asking questions, or heading for the stairwell, back and to the left. The calendar of events here was mind-boggling, though in that way descriptive of our ideal gay life. Tea dances for lesbian ex-nuns, S&M bisexual support groups, gay estate planning, bring-your-own-Barbra Streisand nights...the Center was nothing if not a democracy of sensibilities. Plus there were the weekly meetings for such political organizations as the Gay & Lesbian Anti-Violence Project and the Gay Independent Democrats, as well as all the self-help groups... including AA and Al-Anon and their offshoots into addictions to drugs, food and sex of all kinds. When I first read the twelve-step listing I imagined that people had come up with every possible permutation of every affliction according to every racial, geographical or professional grouping, not to mention minute gradations of sexual preference. I found it extremely funny at the same time that it wasn't...because I didn't know anyone, gay or straight, who wasn't trying to recover from half the things that had happened to them.

I recalled my friend Valerie going to the Center for lesbian Al-Anon and, by mistake, ending up at the meeting for Gay Men Who Love Too Much, because it was the right room but the wrong night. She said the whole group was unfriendly, at first, but begged her to stay after they saw how distraught she was. That evening, she sat in a circle of twelve men and told every detail of her love affair with Claudia, an accounts executive at an ad agency, who she later found out had been sleeping with her secretary during the entire six months they were together. Valerie complained that it seemed like such a heterosexual thing to do, but the others in the group told her to grow up. Valerie said it was the first time she'd felt truly better since the breakup, particularly after she heard what had happened to some of those men in the name of love.

Victor and I walked straight ahead, through the double doors into the hall, behind, where Act Up held its meetings. Here a sea of chairs filled with people stretched hundreds deep and wide. People also stood around the perimeter of the room, singly or in pairs. I took in right away, the way everyone's first instinct is gender-related, whatever their sexuality, that maybe a quarter of the crowd was women, the rest men. This group was, to say the least, eclectic. There were executives who'd come from work in pinstripes, women who looked like old lefty mothers from the neighborhood, a lot of teenagers, of both sexes, with their hair bleached up into spikes or cut haphazardly short, in haircuts you knew they'd given themselves. The majority of the crowd was men in their twenties and thirties, wearing mostly bluejeans and T-shirts printed with familiar messages: *Silence Equals Death*, *Godzilla was Gay*, a lithograph of two men kissing.

There were hardly any seats left, by that time, because the meeting was about to start, but by some stroke of luck, Victor found three in the fourth row not too far from the door. We squeezed past people's knees, then put down our jackets and a *Times* I was carrying to hold them.

"You don't think Sydney's actually going to show up, do you?" I asked.

"I don't know," Victor said. "But the last two weeks she has. When I told her you were coming tonight, she was the one who suggested dinner afterwards. She's photographing some fundraiser at the U.N., this afternoon, featuring the Dalai Lama." Victor shrugged, as if meeting the exiled spiritual leader of Tibet was just all in a day's work, which in Sydney's case, we knew it was. "Certainly if she comes, she'll come late," Victor added. "But I thought we'd save a chair, for a little while, just in case."

The truth was, I didn't need to be reminded of the fact that

Sydney, if she came at all, would come late. You don't spend that many years with someone, albeit impossible ones, without knowing her behavior inside out, the same way certain poems from childhood are imprinted for life. Not that you ever know an ex-lover's motivations, any more than you can guess at your own. But I'm sure that if you added up all the hours I spent waiting for Sydney, at my apartment, at her apartment, in restaurants, at parties and movie theaters, even on street corners, it would be a couple of years I lost from my twenties. When I told this to Victor, he paused for a moment from arranging the jackets.

"I suppose that's better," he said, "than waiting for someone you've never met, which is what most of us do."

After that, Victor and I walked up to the double doors, where we'd come in. A line of people stretched back from where stacks of Xeroxes were arranged on three cafeteria tables against the front wall. We joined the line, and suddenly, I think because I stopped moving, I became aware of the level of noise in the room, like static or a steady tide. Everyone around us was talking.

Victor pointed at the stacks and told me that every week people brought in what they'd found...new medical information, status reports on the court cases for past c.d. actions, upcoming demonstrations here and in New Jersey and Washington, all media coverage of AIDS. I walked behind him in line, gathering the different sheets from the tables. As I watched those going before us, brows furrowed as they bent over each stack, it occurred to me how often people, and particularly the ill, are afraid of information. How people in general don't want to know things...even in this age of TVs, faxes, and computers. It was my relationship with Sydney, actually, that taught me that about myself.

It was only a moment after we'd made it back to our row that they started calling the meeting to order. Our seats were five in from the aisle, and we passed, in succession, a man with a clipped salt-and-pepper beard...two high school boys, one Chinese and one Latino, arm in arm while wearing matching T-shirts that said *Racism Sucks*.... then an obese woman about my age in overalls, whose hands, I noticed, were delicate and slender...next to what I considered to be a very attractive woman in her late forties...Jewish, curly dark hair, a skirt. I sat down beside her, and Victor swept past me, lowering himself into the far seat, which left the middle for Sydney.

The meeting began to quiet down. Up front, the two facilitators, a man and a woman, introduced themselves by their first names, Pam and Howard. Both seemed exceedingly relaxed in front of people, and I understood right away that that was the currency in the room. Pam took the tack of trying to be cheerful yet professional, like a bad therapist. I thought she was probably straight, though you can't always tell. Howard, on the other hand, wearing a bandanna over his head, and standing with hips thrust forward, while he clapped to a calypso beat to get everyone's attention, was not. A tall girl in braids stood beside them, signing the proceedings. She couldn't have been more than eighteen, and she had that kind of intensity you see in people who aren't yet used to living, as if reality were some ride in a convertible, top down, with the wind always blowing in your face.

There were general announcements first, as people stood up, one after another...about an upcoming demonstration at the Health Department on Center Street, a comicbook on safe sex that people needed help distributing to junior high students, an outreach meeting of the *Women & AIDS* newsletter. With each new speaker, the teen-age interpreter seemed to take on a different personality.

"This should be an interesting meeting," Victor leaned across the empty seat to tell me. "There was an argument last week that got so upsetting that one man started crying. Almost half the room threatened to walk out. They were supposed to have a vote, but things got so ugly they put it off till tonight. I think that's why there's so many people here," Victor added, "...for the vote."

"Well, what were they going to vote about?" I asked.

"It's complicated because it's about a split in the organization's thinking about itself more than the actual issue," Victor said. "But, basically, it had to do with whether or not we should send an Act Up delegation to the anti-nuclear march in November."

"But why would someone cry over that?" I asked.

"Because he's dying," Victor said. This made perfect sense. "I'm sure the vote will come up at the top," he added, "because the only other major item on the agenda is the kiss-in."

"Let's see," I said, "I was once at a be-in and also at a smoke-in. But never a kiss-in. It sounds like the sexually explicit version of a love-in," I added, "though, actually, those were about a philosophy of living more than anything else."

"Now Barry wants to make an announcement," Pam roused herself up front, hopping down from the desk where she'd been sitting with her bluejeaned legs outstretched. She walked over to join Howard, who was standing a few yards away, readjusting his bandanna in the reflection from the blackboard.

"Who's Barry?" I whispered over the empty chair.

"I can't remember," Victor said. "But I'm sure I'll recognize him. The same people talk over and over...and about the same things. It's like a weekly soap opera, in which eventually you get back to everyone's plotline."

"Do *you* ever say anything?" I asked.

"Most of what gets discussed here seems beyond comment," he said. HIV positive himself, Victor had yet to show any symptoms.

At that point, something started happening over in the corner, by the two bathrooms at the back of the hall, and we turned around, along with several hundred other people, to see what it was. Suddenly, one of the bathroom doors burst open, and someone started running along the far aisle, away from the street side of the building. It was a man. He was wearing a low-cut strapless dress and clutching what at first I took to be a purse but then realized was a small paperback book. Applause built as he reached the front, a little wobbly, but creditable, on a pair of high heels.

"That's Barry...I recognize him," Victor said. "But just barely. You'd never have expected this. He usually gives the most bland, impersonal presentations...about computer models for cross-referencing drug trials, statistical analyses of the kinds of articles that appear about AIDS in the *Wall Street Journal*, things like that. Frankly, nothing like this has ever happened before," Victor added. "Act Up meetings are never like this." He shook his head, starting to laugh. Everyone else was laughing now, too.

The girl who was signing looked perplexed, for the first time all evening her body as if it had come unplugged, until abruptly her shoulders swung into a kind of rhythm that I thought quite accurately approximated Barry's...because that, of course, was where he carried his intention, in those shoulders revealed by the dress, like a moon unexpectedly glimpsed in daylight. It was instructive, watching a woman impersonate a man who was impersonating a woman.

Barry jumped in his dress to the desk where Pam had just been sitting, then produced a pair of glasses, arched like little wings, which he put on, before flourishing his paperback. I could see from where we sat that it was *Out on a Limb*, the spiritual autobiography of an actress that I actually had read a few years before. For my own part, I believed it was entirely possible that, as the narrative described, friendly aliens had landed in Machu Picchu to contact a New Age movie star...because, honestly, who else *could* they contact?

"Hi, I'm Shirley MacLaine," Barry said and waved. By this time people were waving back and yelling out things like "Hi, Shirley," "Take it off" and "Om shanti." For some reason, I started thinking that there was probably a government informer in the room who was going to have to report all this back to someone. I wondered what they would make of Barry's display, in a political context...if it would be considered a sophisticated form of subversion or simple degeneracy.

Barry wasn't wearing a wig or makeup, nothing to make him appear female beyond the dress and high heels. With a slight beard at the end of the day, the masculine curl of his muscles above the satin, his hair almost a crewcut, he looked exactly like what he was...a man in a dress. You see that in the theater sometimes, when casting goes awry, how some actors save their performances by giving up trying to *be* a character to simply *playing* him. It's the opposite of method acting...as if the audience could be counted on to know that, in life too, there's only roles we step into, or not. Marilyn Monroe used to act like that...and Charlie Chaplain, too. They were always playing themselves playing someone else. That's something gay people know about.

"I've come here to tell you all to love one another," Barry said next. You could tell he was getting into it, the way he kept smiling and tossing his head as if there were long hair attached to it. "Now let's not have a repeat of what happened last week," he continued. "From here on, let's discuss this issue without animosity and without rancor." He looked in his element there on the desk, though that would be a lot of people's idea of torture, mine too, having to stand up in front of five hundred people and impersonate Shirley MacLaine.

There was something about the fact that Barry was enjoying himself so much that started to make everyone else enjoy themselves, too. All around us, you could feel a general loosening up, a release of energy. For a moment, two girls standing near the door danced without music before once again leaning back against a radiator.

"And above all," Barry said after that, "be kind to one another...because there's only one reason we're put here on earth...and that's to love each other."

Barry beckoned to Pam and Howard, who helped him down off the desk in his heels, before ceremoniously escorting him across the front of the room. People applauded while the three of them exited grandly through the door. Then there was a funny silence, as if something were over, but no one quite knew what.

"That was a stroke of genius," Victor said, a moment later. "There would have been no other way to talk about what happened last week without causing it to happen all over again. But now the air is cleared. It was like calling time-out, so for a little while people would have permission not to act as themselves, to let go of petty self-interest. Who knew about that Barry..." he trailed off.

Pam and Howard returned. The actual discussion about whether Act Up should send a delegation to the anti-nuclear rally in November went rather quickly, and for the most part, without animosity or rancor, as Barry had wished. One after another, people rose and spoke for or against the resolution. The basic argument against, made exclusively by men, I was sorry though not surprised to see, was that Act Up's mission was separate from those of all other politically oriented groups and social causes, that none of those groups really cared that gay men were dying, so why should they care about them. That to send a delegation would be to dissipate energy needed exclusively to fight AIDS. On the other side were both men and women, one of whom said that if the whole world blew up AIDS was a moot point. Really, that's what the end of this century had become: a series of races against catastrophe. People pitting wrong against wrong...competing for attention in the media, for private time and public money.

The last person to speak was the woman beside me. There was this satisfying slowness to her movements as she stood up, arranging the folds of her skirt, then leaned on the chair-back in front of her. You could tell she'd paid careful attention to her appearance, and in a room where in general the style of dress was casual and decidedly youthful...featuring T-shirts and tight-fitting jeans on both sexes...it was clear that she stood there as a woman, not a girl. I found this erotic in and of itself.

It turned out she was a social worker at St. Vincent's, specializing in AIDS home care, so she said she knew exactly what was at stake in turning attention away from the issues of cure and treatment. On the other hand, building coalitions with like-minded constituencies was often effective in getting issues addressed at all. You could tell she'd been active in this kind of grassroots politics before, no doubt feminism, because she didn't take anything personally and didn't get excited as she spoke. It was this calm that made her so persuasive, as she mentioned all the other groups that were going to participate in the rally...NOW, Planned Parenthood, Jesse Jackson's Rainbow Coalition, the United Federation of Teachers, the list went on. She drew connections among the aims of several groups, and actually, I think she was just saying out loud what everyone already knew. Maybe that's what was really bothering so many of those men—having found out from the foot-dragging response to the AIDS epidemic that they were valued as little as the rest of us. It came to a vote right after that. The resolution passed.

Just then I caught the wave of someone's hand from the corner of my eye, and something in my body shifted. But when I turned fully around, I saw that it wasn't Sydney. I was disappointed at the same time that I was relieved.

"I think we better give up the seat. It's already eight," Victor said, then beckoned for the man standing at the end of our row to come in. Everyone rearranged themselves as he brushed by us to seat himself between Victor and me. He was wearing glasses and a natty cardigan sweater...the sensitive intellectual type. He deposited a briefcase on his lap and opened it. Inside, he glanced at something that I thought looked like a script.

The remaining item on the agenda was the kiss-in, scheduled for that Thursday evening, at rush hour, in Sheraton Square. It was a sort of guerilla action, it turned out, at which people were supposed to go stand in traffic and kiss members of the same sex. This did not sound like my cup of tea. On the other hand, it was true that a lot of the time, in public, I was careful with my body around Helen, even when I wasn't conscious of it. Not that you can hide anything. A salesgirl in a boutique, once, trying to make sense of the way we touched each other, when I was trying on a suit, asked if Helen and I were sisters, her large-breasted Eastern European body, bold facial features and dark hair next to my blondeness, blue eyes, body closer to a boy's. It was only when we told her yes that she realized she'd asked the wrong question.

The people who were organizing the kiss-in had to leave early, so Pam and Howard were put in charge. I'd grown rather fond of them, in spite of myself, by this time. They reminded me of TV anchors, who at least in New York always come in pairs, male and female. There was also the issue of having to report bad news, but breezily. Here we were in a meeting that ultimately had to do with fighting a condition from which people simply didn't recover. On the other hand, this was also a definition of life.

Pam announced, next, that we were going to practice. On the other side of the man between us, I caught Victor's eye. He shrugged, as if to relinquish responsibility, once and for all, for anything else that might happen that night. The crowd was buzzing.

"We're just going to pass kisses across each row." Howard took the initiative next. "Does everyone know how to do that?" There was general laughter. I realized the last time I'd had to do anything like this was at interactive events in the sixties, when, in the name of social change, it had seemed honorable to do everything asked of you.

From where I sat, the physical action looked like one of those waves they do in the stands at a football game, only with a crucial difference. Within about two minutes, a kiss had been sent from the front, across each row, from side to side, to the back of the room and forward again. The woman beside me was polite though impersonal, both times, the man quite a bit more animated. I added that evening to the list of the more screwball events I'd participated in, in my life, though, considering the time I grew up in, that list was quite long.

"You know that guy who was sitting between us?" Victor said, once we were outside again. We were headed east on Thirteenth Street, toward the Japanese restaurant on Seventh Avenue.

"Yes," I said, "the one with the glasses and the cardigan sweater. What about him?"

"Well, I thought maybe that if I saw him, again, next week, I'd ask him out," Victor answered. "That is, if I felt up to facing rejection, in case he said no. His name is Ed Moss, and he's the receptionist at that gay high school...you know, the one they fundraise for all the time. I read it on some papers in his briefcase," Victor admitted. Then he looked closely at me, as if I might reveal something in my face that wouldn't be there in my words. This was entirely possible.

"Why not?" I said, trying to sound optimistic, the way you have to with your friends on the topic of romance. "I thought he looked very sensitive, and also"—Here I pulled out all the stops—"I thought he was a good kisser."

"I thought so, too," Victor agreed, getting that look people do when they've just met somebody, and the world as we know it...of other commitments, specific sexual habits, divergent intellectual interests and upbringing, the tyranny of toilet training, call it the impossible undertow of the past... momentarily ceases to exist. I thought of the number of times in my own life I'd kissed a stranger with such hopes. One of them had been Sydney, who, Victor and I decided later, had probably gone to dinner with the Dalai Lama.

It was Indian Summer, one of the few seasons you can still count on in this era of apocalyptic weather. The last few days had turned beautiful and mild, for October, and that Friday they'd gotten a good turnout for the demonstration at the Health Department. When I got off the M-15 bus, around four, there were already about two hundred picketers behind police barriers. Having skipped the kiss-in, Victor and I had sworn to meet for this.

Patrolmen lined the street and steps of the building, where I knew, later, the civil disobedience was going to happen. You could tell the group was well-organized because of the high-tech cardboard signs people carried, with two-color lithography and professional printing. "And I am Marie of Rumania," one sign said. "And I am Marilyn Monroe," said another. On the reverse side of both, I saw after a moment, was the photograph of a well-known closeted politician, who'd been quoted the week before as saying, "I am a heterosexual." Since AIDS it was considered everyone's duty to come out, like it or not.

Most of the crowd was male...handsome boys in t-shirts and older men in suits. But there were several women there, too...radical girls in their twenties with most of their hair shaved off, nose rings...people's mothers trying to look brave in the face of insupportable grief...and friends, most of whom were lesbians, which though it may not have been obvious to the average passerby, was obvious to me.

I didn't see Victor in the loop of people that extended for half a block up the sidewalk in front of the building, so I just took a sign from a stack next to the curb and stepped under the barricades. Mine featured two columns of numbers, Act Up's versus the Health Department's, regarding diagnosed AIDS cases in New York City and New York State, and community hospital and hospice beds, projected and available, as of the first of September. What struck me about all of the handouts, and many of the other signs, too, was how statistical the information was. It reminded me of Vietnam, with its constant revision of government figures...of casualties, wounded, landmines, battalions, M-16s, Viet Cong...none of which any of us trusted, and rightly. It suddenly made sense to me that an illness, like a career or a lover or a war, would change the methodology of people's thinking...how they organize and make sense of what happens to them. A few of the men looked sick, their hair like long peach fuzz, the way you imagine babies with a whole life ahead of them. You knew that in any group like this, several of the healthy-looking men were dying, too.

Just then a cab pulled up, and Sydney stepped out of it. As usual, she looked late for an extremely important appointment...a wallet clutched in one hand, her camera thrown over her shoulder, pressed white shirt over too-short tights and a pair of sneakers. It was part of her charm, as if she were too busy and life too interesting to find clothes that fit or a bag to hold her belongings. She didn't see me, and I watched as James, who had hosted Victor's fortieth birthday party the year before, got out the curbside door after her. He was dressed similarly now to the way he had been that night I met him, in a suit and expensive accessories. He was a literary agent, who specialized mostly in celebrities.

James was the last person I expected to see at a demonstration, and it occurred to me I should have been surprised to see Sydney, too. But I knew Victor had probably told her that he'd be there, and it wasn't so farfetched that a photographer would show up on such a day. Actually, I realized, I was never surprised to see Sydney, which may have had something to do with the fact that I saw her every day for so many years, a reality that doesn't quite leave your thinking, even after the person does.

Sydney didn't seem surprised to see me either, as I stepped out of the picketline and touched her elbow. We kissed hello, in a way that was intimate but reserved, before she introduced me again to James. At that moment, Victor called to us, then parted from the line himself. It turned out that he'd been just a dozen people behind me. The two of us marvelled that we hadn't seen each other in the half hour we'd been marching around.

The c.d. was planned for 5:00, when people got off work and employees of the Health Department would be trying to go home. Victor, James and I carried signs in front of the building for the next fifteen minutes, while Sydney took photographs. Then, I noticed, she moved over to get a good spot by the entrance, and just stood there, her gaze riveted until the action would start. How well I remembered that concentration that once upon a time, for years, really, was trained on me, then on her work, until I could never seem to get enough of her time, and finally on another woman, who was younger than I was and sillier, not that any of that mattered. You realize personalities are the least of it when something like that happens.

The people who sat down on the steps of the Health Department at five o'clock looked determined, though almost casual, as they linked arms and prepared to settle in. A kind of formal procedure followed, as intricate as certain social conventions of the past, during which time the police asked the demonstrators to move, which they didn't, informed them they'd be arrested, which they knew, then proceeded to break the human chain. War whoops and cries of "Shame!" erupted from the crowd of onlookers, which included us.

Just a few feet away, Sydney was taking photographs. I think it was our proximity that caused some old landscape of feeling to return. Suddenly, it seemed to me that the two of us were on a high plain, windswept and alone, everything else of meaning in the world hidden below a horizon. Unlike Helen, Sydney was shorter than I was, and though not thin, even fleshy, was compact in a way that made me want to walk up and encircle her with my arms. She had a kind of energy I'd always wanted to contain. It was a physical thing, beyond my control or intention. I would probably always feel that way about her.

Inside the lobby of the building, on the other side of revolving doors, stood a growing crowd of people who couldn't get out. They looked disgusted and angry, which I could understand. That's what comes from living in New York, where there are more moral dilemmas in a day than some other places confront you with in a year. Several businessmen and -women passing on the sidewalk beyond the police barriers stopped to look at the demonstrators being dragged to a nearby paddy wagon, but others just hurried by. I guess that's really why Victor and I had come that afternoon, simply to go on record as having stopped our lives, temporarily, in the face of disaster. It's a small thing.

By that time, a lot of the people had gone home, or been arrested, so that there were only about fifty of us left to finish off the demonstration, which was supposed to end at City Hall. We walked the few blocks, then up behind the back of that building, alongside a green. I don't know exactly why, but it felt otherworldly, like some odd funeral procession, or the dance of the dead, as we walked forward, Victor next to James, myself with Sydney, near the end of a straggly line. Obviously, it had to do with the disease itself. But there was something also about the fact that the sidewalks were empty, the downtown work force having cleared out immediately after five, because it was a Friday, and the weather so beautiful, so unexpectedly. Actually, it felt like being the last people on earth, a feeling I've always equated with love, because of the hiddenness of an earlier part of my life.

We were directed by a marshall to stop in front of a monument, where our depleted numbers bunched up to listen to a final rally in the gathering dusk. The monument was the bronze statue of a World War I soldier, with familiar accoutrements: from the base up...high boots, knickers, buttoned jacket, rifle with bayonet, helmet.

The first speaker jumped up on the base and made his remarks holding onto the soldier's waist, as he would a lover's. He said he'd been arrested for civil disobedience fourteen times that year. An activist, he had that glassy-eyed look you saw in draft-age boys who'd quit school or their jobs during Vietnam to work against the war, then slowly became immobilized by their task. Frankly, he seemed pretty much off the deep end. But I figured that was his business. People do what they need to to go forward, to paint a kind of canvas of life onto which they can then picture themselves walking. Like

Sydney and myself in the beginning, the kind of physical invincibility you feel when falling in love...how near the end with her I felt like some broken-down horse...slow on my feet, sway-backed, no longer handsome.

It was right after that, that another young man, in an immaculate gray suit, got up to speak. He chose to stand at the feet of the soldier, the statue above and behind him, like a parent or a memory...history, which is what it was. After that, he began reading from a list of upcoming actions for November...in a monotone, not ever looking up. It was such a contrast to the energy of the man before him, who though manic, at least had seemed alive.

"Do you know who that is?" Victor stepped next to me to ask. James had moved to the side to have a cigarette, and Sydney was still roaming around taking pictures. The crowd, in general, looked bored but were curiously patient with the presentation.

"No," I said. "Who?"

"Barry," Victor answered. I shook my head, looking forward again.

"You can't be serious," I told Victor. The young man in the suit was almost completely without affect as he continued, as if speaking a language he didn't know. The owlish glasses on his face were nothing like the plastic wings he'd worn as Shirley MacLaine, when he'd been so happy, so animated, so himself.

"I know," said Victor. "It seems impossible...but that's Barry." He paused before continuing, "Isn't it amazing...how what motivates people on a deeper level is so seldom the way they present themselves in the world?"

"It's a comment on the strangeness of the human heart," I said.

A few minutes later, we settled into a booth at the *Captain's Quarters*, the only bar we'd found open within a three-block radius of City Hall. The demonstration was over, and it turned out that Victor, James and Sydney were all going away together for the weekend, with Sydney's current lover, but not until seven. So we'd decided to have a drink.

"Is this OK for everyone?" Victor asked.

Sydney nodded, a woman whose material possessions could be fit into a single trunk, and had been several times, as she'd changed lovers and apartments and lives. James looked down at the paper placemats, which concordant with the nautical theme of the restaurant, showed how to tie various knots. The atmosphere was a little déclassé for the likes of him. But he rose to the occasion.

"It's fine," he said. Victor nodded, then the waitress came over, a woman in her fifties who'd worked too hard for too little money, no doubt for too long, but had retained her graciousness. The three of them ordered martinis, which, though Sydney looked over at me to see how I was taking that news, was no indisposition at all. I hadn't seriously wanted a drink in the five years since I quit the last time.

After the waitress returned with our drinks, we started talking about the Dalai Lama. Sydney said that after the U.N. meeting, there was a press conference at the Hilton, where afterwards she'd been able to get close to him. For months, she'd been doing a series of portraits of famous people, which James was going to package, later, as a book. Not celebrities, necessarily, but people who'd done something worthwhile.

"Did he look holy to you?" I asked Sydney.

"He did," she answered, "though whether that came from something innate he was born with, or was the result of having been chosen, I can't say." This was typical Sydney, metaphysical though inconclusive.

"How do they pick the Dalai Lama?" James asked after that, and neither Sydney nor Victor knew. But I remembered something about the Tibetan equivalent of wise men, i.e., the most exalted of the Buddhist monks, going to people's homes to look for his reincarnated spirit almost immediately after the death of the last Dalai Lama. By performing a series of tests and divinations they found the right boy, who later would serve for life.

"It sounds so mystical," Sydney said, "but since the current Dalai Lama was installed in 1940—then in 1959, after the Chinese installed their own rival leader, exiled to India—his whole life has been politics.

"Do you know what the direct translation of *Dalai Lama* is?" Sydney asked the company at large. We shook our heads. "*Ocean-wide superior one*," she said.

"Well, that puts it in no uncertain terms," Victor replied. "Actually, it makes me think of my mother."

"Can you imagine trying to live up to a name like that?" James pondered.

"But if you look at it from another perspective," I said, "he doesn't have to live up to anything. He *is* that from the moment that he's chosen. He's automatically who he is." You could tell everyone liked this idea, in a culture and a life where we were always struggling to know who we were.

"What a wonderful state of mind that must make for," Victor commented. "It's the opposite of existentialism, of modernism, of Descartes', '*Je pense, donc je suis.*' No wonder they're celibate," he added, "because from that perspective there's no need for sex, either. You're already in a kind of equilibrium with yourself." After a moment, James called for the check.

We walked out into the night. It was still warm, though the temperature had dropped some with the loss of the sun. To tell the truth, it seemed strange that the three of them should be going off without me, that weekend, because I knew that in some parallel life, in which I would be myself but still with Sydney, I'd be going, too. Suddenly, my old lover started dashing up the street after a cab, but then retraced her paces, having failed to stop it. I'd felt that way once about her.

I think I would have done anything Sydney asked, at a certain point. The problem was, she didn't ask. Two things stand out in my mind on the topic of not wanting to know, which struck me so forcefully at the Act Up meeting: the pictures I discovered in Sydney's wallet of her and some other woman in Paris together that winter I passed my orals, when she was supposedly on a shoot, and the phone call at my apartment, the next summer, from the unidentified friend who, not knowing who I was or where he had called, asked first for Sydney, then for Sasha, which was the first time I'd heard her name, before informing me that he'd try them at the house in East Hampton. The world is full of mysteries, most as unresolvable as how they choose the Dalai Lama. But that explained, quite definitively, why Sydney had had to work so many weekends. Honestly, you ask yourself, like Shirley MacLaine must have at first with those aliens, Am I crazy?

Or reverse the subjectivity, how the aliens, who'd been hidden from the human eye, revealed themselves, to of all people, Shirley MacLaine. But why not Shirley MacLaine? You pick who you pick, through a series of tests and divinations, though no one quite knows what those are.

The question remained, would I do it over again, knowing the outcome? Let's just say that like the Dalai Lama, we'd all prefer to be chosen for life.

Suddenly, Sydney called out to me. She'd found another cab. After that, the four of us drove uptown, not talking much. They ended up dropping me on Eighth Street, and I began walking east toward Helen's, where in this life, at least, I knew I belonged.

Surviving High School

That morning, I was the last person on the crosstown bus. Not a lot of people go to Christopher Street and the river, a prime cruising ground, at 10:15 AM. As I climbed down, I said goodbye to the driver I'd gotten once before at that hour. Since Victor had started dating Ed Moss, I'd been volunteering at the gay high school. On sabbatical that year, I had time for once.

It was gray, the way November is in New York, and raining. En route to the school, a block away, I passed a Chinese restaurant, a coffee shop, and an S&M boutique, whose paraphernalia in the window looked, before noon, like objects from another planet. As I climbed the steps that opened directly off of West Street, the stairway looked newly vaulted, with its coat of white paint. They'd been renovating the three-story brownstone, little by little. It still needed a lot of work, but had been an outright donation they couldn't refuse.

When I told my friends, a month earlier, that I was going to teach at the gay high school, most of them wondered what that was. All of us had just been educated with everyone else, and at a time in history when, if you were gay, you certainly didn't want anyone to know. As it turned out, I didn't really understand what a gay high school was, myself. But riding up in the elevator, the day of my interview, with two teenage drag queens, outfitted in wigs and silicone breasts, I began to have some inkling.

Sonia, the social worker I met with that afternoon, tried to discourage me. The two of us sat in a cubicle formed from three-quarter partitions...one of a dozen the staff occupied in the largest, middle room of the floor they had then, in a small office building on Twenty-third Street, before the imminent move downtown. Up front, where I'd come in, was the director's office and an alcove used as the reception area, where that morning, Sonia told me, someone had stolen the lunch...forty sandwiches, three dozen milks, two half-gallon jars of fruit salad...not to mention the bagels, orange juice, and a week's supply of jam left over from breakfast. In the back, to which she pointed after that, was the classroom, where a knife fight had broken out the day before. I think I was more surprised that there was only one classroom than that boys had been fighting amongst themselves.

Having informed me of the week's catastrophes, Sonia returned both hands to her pockets, then sat back, spreading her legs in a gesture that I associate, and not positively, with men. After that, she referred to gay adults as role models, then spoke for a while about the students, with their variety of clinical disorders, from which most of them would never recover. I found this description of life so awful that by the time she asked why I wanted to teach there, I'd almost decided not to.

It wasn't what I'd expected, mostly black and Puerto Rican *boys*, several of them transvestites, at least from the waist up...everyone now wore bluejeans...though it occurred to me later that what I'd imagined ahead of time was simply myself at their age, in boarding school, when I first began to realize that I fell in love with girls instead of boys, that being around women's bodies made me want to touch them.

I tried explaining my reasons to Sonia, who as a Puerto Rican woman, and one who'd grown up in poverty, seemed skeptical. But I think she liked me better for having no clear idea of my mission when she was so sure about her own. Afterwards, she just looked at me for a moment, nodded, then asked for three letters of reference. In the end, I wasn't sure whether it was being a lesbian or a professor that qualified me.

What struck me most about that first afternoon of my interview was the classroom...bright like a birdcage it had so many windows, but small, the size of an apartment dining room...and Erin, one of the two teachers they had, looking like some deposed prince, androgynous in overalls by the door. I was surprised to see that there were only about a dozen students, sitting at those old-fashioned armed desks. They were taking a proficiency test, and sat chewing their pencils, crossing and uncrossing their legs, writing with a flourish, then looking off into space. It seemed impossible that these were the same kids Sonia had described in her office just a few doors away. But soon enough I came to understand that other energy that would shut them down and turn them against everyone, including themselves. They were like sailors on a ship barely seaworthy, whose solution was to save themselves by jumping overboard.

For the rest of that afternoon, we wrote and delivered monologues. It was a class the more flamboyant types enjoyed, because it allowed for dramatic presentations of self, and even the shyer members felt it was their chance to try out important new identities...which is what the theater, and all of art, is for. One diminutive girl, who spoke and wrote only in Spanish, which I didn't understand, insisted on reading her monologue aloud to me. We worked on gestures and body language, and I could feel in the way she settled into my touch, like a cat, how desperately she needed a woman's attention. Theresa, a transvestite so convincing in feminine mannerisms that at first I'd actually mistaken her for some peculiar throwback of a girl, tried to imitate the heroines of TV shows...like "Dallas" and "Falcon Crest." It took me a while to understand that some density of *self* I was looking to work with in these students was, in many cases, not within their reach. Who they really were was locked behind a door neither they nor I knew how to open.

A sign on the second-floor landing of the new brownstone said *Drop-in Center*. I pressed the bell and was buzzed in. From his seat behind a newly glassed-in reception booth, Ed Moss made a Roman salute with the telephone. In his other hand, he held a copy of *Romeo and Juliet*, in which he was playing the lead at a church in Park Slope. Ed was one of those young actors who live for the theater, who pick day jobs solely for congeniality and the time to memorize lines. I was getting to know him at the same time Victor was, albeit in a different way.

"You must be a week into rehearsal now," I said, pointing at his script. "How's it going?"

"Better," Ed answered, then leaned forward, quoting, "'Is love a tender thing? It is too rough, too rude, and too boisterous, and it pricks like a thorn.'"

"That *is* better," I said, and he recited a few more lines.

The last time I'd been there, he and I had talked for an hour about the motivation of Romeo. It was touching how much of himself he put into a role that would be seen by, at most, a few hundred people. I thought of the number of actors I'd known who put everything they had into obscure roles in obscure productions. There were worse things you could do with your life.

The waiting room, whose old plaid couch looked shabby against the newly constructed wall of the reception booth, was empty. I walked along the corridor, past the offices of the social workers, where most of the doors were open, and these were empty, too. On my way back, I knocked on the glass. Ed mouthed "Come in," and as I walked around and into the booth, small as a cockpit, with its one back window facing the river, he was just hanging up the phone. It seemed funny, walking across a threshold that just a week ago hadn't been there.

"Where is everyone?" I asked Ed.

"You mean the staff?" he said, turning in his swivel chair. "They're all in a meeting across the hall."

Ed pointed at the closed door of the Drop-in Center. Formerly a large windowless storage area, it had been renovated into a kind of rec room for the kids in the afternoons. With its Ping-Pong table, ancient TV on legs, a half-dozen fold-up chairs, scattered ashtrays, and pine-paneled walls, it looked like somebody's basement from the fifties.

"So how did *you* get out of going?" I asked.

"Somebody had to man the phones," Ed said.

Actually, this was crucial. The high school, and the institute that contained it, served gay youth not only in New York City but all over the state and beyond. Every day the switchboard was lighted with calls from desperate teenagers...in Texas, California, Missouri...most of whom had no one at home or among their friends and teachers whom they could safely tell they were gay. The social workers would talk to them at length, sometimes referring them to groups or counselors in their own area. There were also packets of information ready to mail, if that could be done without risk of self-incrimination...on safe sex, legal rights for minors, things like that...though a lot of the advice they gave was simply survival techniques until the kids turned eighteen and could legally leave home. These included such strategies as stealing books on homosexuality from the library, so you wouldn't have to sign them out, and tips for high school dating, like going steady with the least sexual person in your class.

"So what's today's agenda?" I asked, nodding in the direction of the Drop-in Center.

"*Homophobia*," Ed answered, then rolled his eyes. Gregory, the director, had been involved at Essalen in the sixties, and the staff was always having to discuss such topics as that...should we call the drag queens *him* or *her*...self-hatred in our daily lives.

"I don't know how anybody stands it," I said.

"They can't stand it," he replied. "But the social workers beat everybody down. It's like in China...people have to go around in a circle and criticize themselves."

The phone rang again, and Ed answered it. I walked out into the hall and up the stairs. Though the social workers had offices below, the high school shared this top floor with the staff for the other support services...Martin, the ex-priest, who found housing for the students who'd either been thrown out by their families or were runaways...Clarice, who was often interviewed on local news shows about AIDS education, which was her specialty...and Arthur, the serious and bespectacled fundraiser, who in another mental lifetime had been married and worked at the Ford Foundation.

Both in the larger classroom, whose door was open, and the smaller one, which was more like a large closet, its top half glass, everyone sat huddled in their coats. This meant that the heating system had broken down again. I waved as several of the students in Oliver's classroom called out my name. They were probably glad to see me, but the larger truth was, they'd respond to any interruption.

After that, I walked into the smaller classroom, where Erin was tutoring the special ed students. I heard a sound, which I recognized right away as water dripping. With the rain, the roof had sprung its usual leaks, and you could see buckets scattered around the floor. Once again, confused priorities seemed the story of life...here we were with a leaky roof and no heat, and the staff was in a meeting about homophobia.

You could hear Oliver call break in the other room. Immediately, his and Erin's students thundered downstairs to smoke cigarettes, one of their favorite pastimes. That's when Erin began telling me about how, during first period, Ramon had gone unconscious, from too much crack. They'd had to break down the bathroom door, then carry him off to St. Vincent's. I walked to where she was pointing. With the door still off, you could see directly into the tiled interior. The scene looked eerie, like the aftermath of a small tornado.

Erin and Oliver and I spent the next ten minutes talking about Ramon. For more than a year, he'd been off crack and the streets, where he'd hustled at night in the meat markets. He was the only student there who read real books, like *For Whom the Bell Tolls, A Tree Grows in Brooklyn, Jane Eyre.*

Another boy had once described himself and his grandmother as "reading" in their living room, but this had turned out to mean making insults or "throwing shade," another of the students' favorite pastimes. After that, leaving me in charge till lunch, Erin and Oliver went downstairs.

I walked into the larger classroom, whose windows and fire door faced the Hudson, the same as Ed's view below. On a side wall hung a poster of the abolitionist freed slave Frederick Douglass, next to one of Santa Claus dispensing condoms. Opposite, there was a blowup of the Bill of Rights above a beehive of open lockers, which no one used because of theft. What could be seen around that room summed up quite well the complexities of the lives within.

There was no telling who was going to show up when break was over, or if those who did would want to do anything besides gossip and make jokes. The motivation of a few diehard students aside, the bunch of them were more than anything else *teenagers*...obsessed with their appearance, imitative of their peers, quick to fall in and out of love. There was also the attrition rate, of which Ramon was the most recent example.

After an hour of improvisation, Oliver called the students to lunch. Once again, everyone jumped from their seats and thundered downstairs. They were in high spirits, even after the events of the morning, including Ramon. The problem was, they were too used to terrible things happening. Afterwards, I just sat there at the desk. It always took me a while to get over class, in part because the boys were so taxing... because they were boys, with that kind of overbearing adolescent maleness, however they were dressed and however they'd transformed their bodies.

I think it was Helen who told me the three biggest problems in high schools, thirty years ago, when both Kennedys and King were still alive: smoking cigarettes, swearing, and gum chewing, in that order. Well, at the institute they were strictly into survival, trying to rescue kids going down the rabbit hole from AIDS, crack, alcohol, all forms of abuse, self-inflicted and otherwise. This was before even the idea, let alone the ideal, of education could come in. When I mentioned the situation there to a woman I knew who taught tenth grade in the Bronx, she said that, exceptions aside, that's what high school is in this city now.

It made me wonder whatever would become of us...our society...like when you go to the supermarket and none of the cashiers can name any of the vegetables. Or those homeless kids I heard about, whose teacher drew a turkey on the blackboard at Thanksgiving and not one of them knew what it was. Suspicious, she brought in a reference book. It turned out that they'd never seen a lion, a giraffe, or an elephant, not even in pictures.

Three weeks later, it was freezing cold, at 6:00 p.m., on West Street, with the wind blowing off the river. After class, I'd spent the whole afternoon with Ed, going over the fine tuning of his performance. This was a part of the theater I missed, listening to a speech go from being simply words to a character's thoughts and feelings. I remembered an acting teacher I had once, reading an ad for Bonwit's with such intention she might have been putting on those clothes in front of us. The play was opening that Saturday. Victor had gotten us all tickets.

That night, Helen and I were going to Marge and Carol's for dinner. Their apartment at Westbeth, the old telephone company building that was converted in the sixties to artists' residences, was only a couple of blocks away. I had an hour to kill before meeting Helen at the subway. So I went to the Peacock Cafe, where I had a cappuccino and read the *Times*...what I now thought of as somehow old-fashioned pursuits.

By the time I walked over to Sheridan Square and stood near the cigar store above the subway exit, it was after seven. But I knew Helen wouldn't be on time. She would have started reading something at work, then just gotten lost in it or looked into a store window uptown, on the way to the subway, and somehow or other found herself going in. It was this powerful sense of curiosity, in which the world existed simply to be looked at, taken in, that had attracted me to Helen in the first place. I'd wanted her to take me in in that way, too.

About quarter after seven, Helen came up the stairs of the subway. I put away the magazine I'd been reading by streetlight. As usual, she was loaded down, carrying a tote bag as well as her purse, and tonight a third bag, filled with a by-now-familiar inventory: magazines, a Walkman, music tapes, gum, bagels, a flashlight, extra batteries, probably even a screwdriver.

"So how was your class?" she asked, kissing me. "Did anyone show up?"

"Yes," I said. "About eight students, the same as last time. But I don't know about those kids...if it does any good. There are certain basic concepts, like what's real and what isn't, that some of them still don't get. For example, Theresa"—I'd told Helen about her and all the students—"didn't know the difference between a soap opera and a documentary. We had to go over the difference between a person being an actress as her profession and playing a character, who, in most cases, has a different profession." I shook my head. "She thought the nurses on the TV show *General Hospital* were actually nurses..."

"Most people are overcommitted to reality," Helen said. I thought this was a sweet way of looking at it.

I lifted Helen's extra bag onto my shoulder, and the two of us crossed at the light on Christopher Street. We started walking on West Fourth, past the gym that had once been for men but was now for women, and the empty outdoor seats of the Riviera Cafe, where I must have eaten hundreds of meals in my twenties, most of them after midnight. Walking in the Village was like the moment before death, in which all of your life comes back to you.

"It's just that being their teacher, I'm supposed to help them find their place in the world," I told Helen. "Mrs. Bloom, in boarding school, did that for me."

I could still picture those art history classes, where we spent weeks with the lights off, watching slide after slide of Michelangelos, Da Vincis, Botticellis. Mrs. Bloom, our teacher, would sit in the back, transfixed, sometimes not saying a word for the whole two hours. Some of the girls slept during that period, their torsos in shadow on the desks. But I remember how beautiful those paintings were, like some wallpaper to a room in my mind, where I'm still a girl and all the things that have happened since then to change me haven't yet.

At the time, what struck me was how unencumbered Mrs. Bloom was by public opinion, how little she needed anyone else's approbation or permission to do what she pleased. As a young woman she'd lost a son, who was handicapped for all of his short life, and people said she was thinking about him as she sat in the back of the classroom. But I thought of it differently, as if the loss of the son had opened her more fully to the paintings.

"Mrs. Bloom was dedicated to the point of having very little life of her own," I recalled. "She was divorced, by then, and her son had died. On weekends, she used to take us on tours of the Boston Museum of Fine Arts or the Isabela Stewart Gardener Collection, which a friend of hers would open privately for us, after hours. At first, it was eerie walking through those rooms without anyone else in sight. But later," I told Helen, "it seemed natural to be alone with the art. To this day when I go into a museum and other people are there, it doesn't seem right."

"You poor privileged girl," she said, ruffling my hair.

"Cut it out," I told her. We'd had this sort of interchange before.

"I never had a great teacher," Helen reflected after a moment, "unless you count fashion design school, where a certain meticulous attention over months and years constituted a kind of greatness. Designers like St. Laurent and Oscar de la Renta would come in for an afternoon's critique, while our regular teachers would sit with us for six hours a day, five days a week...retracing patterns, draping material, tearing out stitches.

"They were professionals," Helen said, "in the old sense of the word, and they prided themselves on that. But in high school," she added, "our teachers were hardly competent and in some cases not. Those people simply wanted to get out at the end of the day and go home to their families. They had no mission or calling. They were earning a living."

"What a shame," I said.

"It was a farce," Helen corrected me. "For example," she said, "my junior year, they didn't have enough French teachers to go around...because they'd underhired for the system. So, in our school, where they had an extra typing teacher, they just made one of them teach French. Of course, there was the small matter that the woman couldn't *speak* French," Helen continued. "But she would just read one lesson ahead, and teach us that in class the next day. If anybody asked a question that was covered further on in the book, they had to wait. And if we wanted to write a composition about something that had already happened or that we wanted to do in the future, she made us pretend it was happening right then... because all any of us knew for months was the present tense."

As a teacher, I found this disgusting; it was a kind of crime against humanity, denying young minds the past and the future. But Helen, whose vision of learning was less exalted than mine, simply shrugged.

"Not only that," she went on, "but we did *Julius Caesar* in English class both freshman and sophomore year. We were supposed to move on to *Macbeth*. But they never ordered it, because of budget cuts...so we just did the other play over again."

"That's an outrage," I voiced my earlier sentiments. "It's against the whole spirit of education." Helen looked thoughtful for a moment.

"In a funny way," she said, "it turned out all right. By the second year, people began to get a feel for the characters and their motivations. And memorizing a hundred lines was a pleasure, because everyone just picked the same ones they had before...and they meant more to us over time. But both teachers taught out of the same study guide, so it got boring, too. We had to discuss the exact same themes, each year, and write a paper on one of three topics..."Hubris," "Betrayal," or "Power Corrupts." I wrote on betrayal, twice, because I knew that was the primary activity of adulthood," Helen said.

"I can't believe how precocious you were," I told her, "particularly since you didn't really have an education."

"Oh, I had an education," Helen said, "but not in school."

We'd arrived at Westbeth, which stretched for a whole block between Washington and West Streets. The building was about equidistant from the high school and the meat markets, where Erin had said Ramon was hustling again. The guard inside the entrance hall waved us over to his table. We walked up and signed in, which is what you always have to do there, but tonight he also called upstairs. Security was tighter since a man had tried to set one of the tenants on fire coming down in an elevator. I can't say this piece of information seemed real to me, as we rode upstairs, right after that. It was like Ramon out hustling in the meat markets...I couldn't quite picture it.

Margery's son Burt opened the apartment door. He said Carol was still in the shower, which we could hear running as we passed by the bathroom into the kitchen. His boyfriend, Rob, who was a jewelry designer, had to meet a deadline that night and wasn't coming, he added, while the two other guests weren't there yet. Burt paused to peer inside the oven.

By the time we'd walked into the back of the one big open room that constituted the apartment, its floor-to-ceiling, eleventh-story windows facing east and downtown, Margery was descending from the sleeping loft. After she kissed Helen and me hello, she stood with her arm around her son, the two of them a happy gay family. They didn't look so different from each other, actually, though Burt wore a beard and glasses, and had recently crewcut his hair, while Margery was a few inches shorter and wider, her bangs now salted with gray. I knew her from my years in the theater.

I mentioned having taught at the high school, that day. People always liked to hear about it, because that's a time in your own life everyone has strong feelings about, and if you're gay, it's double whammy. I recounted a few episodes from the morning...some of them funny, some of them not. Life at the institute was like a cross between a sitcom and Greek tragedy.

This got Helen and Burt talking about their own years in New York public high schools, Helen at a 4,500-student magnet school in Queens in the mid-sixties and Burt an alternative school in Brooklyn in the seventies. The most horrible part for both of them, in those more benign eras, had been sports.

"They didn't make me take any P.E. for three years," Burt said. "But then, when I was a senior, a football coach got promoted to vice principal, and he insisted I make everything up. The funny part was, I'd finished all my academic requirements, so all I took that year was four periods of tap dancing."

Carol, who'd just come out of the bathroom, dressed in a black jumpsuit, kissed Helen and me hello. Her silver hair still wet, her mouth red with lipstick, she looked pretty good for someone old enough to be Burt's mother. So did Burt's mother.

"I used to dream all the time about class...that I was dancing," Burt remembered. "Shuffle ball change...stamp pivot pivot."

Carol lowered her hips to balance on the arm of Margery's chair. Then she bent over to cut a piece of cheese, resting her hand on her lover's shoulder. They'd been together since Carol had left her husband, fifteen years before. Actually, both had been married for decades, the kind of time span they were now working on with each other.

"I had P.E. first thing in the morning, at eight-ten," Helen said. "It was horrible enough to get up at six-thirty to shower, do your hair, put on stockings with a garter belt, bra, skirt, top, and in my case, false eyelashes, without having to take everything off again an hour later. Of course, the first line of defense was to get your period, because then you could sit in the infirmary with the other girls who had it, or said they did, and the ones who'd recently gotten nose jobs. But, obviously you couldn't use that too often."

"Well, what kind of things did you do in gym?" I asked, unable to picture Helen doing any form of athletics or even that girl she must have been.

"Jump around," she answered. "Throw a ball." The words themselves seemed distasteful to her.

Burt started showing us one of his tap routines, which he said were like memories of the body not the mind. That's when the doorbell rang, and Carol walked over to let in the other couple, whom neither Helen nor I, nor Burt, for that matter, had met before. They were closer to Marge and Carol's age than ours, maybe mid-fifties. When they got closer, the stockier one with the dark hair, Bobby...the second woman, Pat, was petite and blonde...immediately started dancing beside Burt.

I know a relentless performer when I see one, and it turned out Marge had met Bobby, years ago, at a community playhouse in Westchester. Though she'd worked less often in her youth, she now got character parts on network television, Marge told us, as Bobby nodded, smiling. The girlfriend, straight from work in pearls and a suit, was a buyer for Bloomingdale's. Very well-preserved for a woman of her age, Pat irritated me, too...though not for that reason. There was just a certain annoying self-satisfaction about both of them.

After that, we moved to the dinner table, where the conversation proceeded, though not brilliantly. At various points in the evening, I felt like picking a fight with both Pat and Bobby, who had continued a nonstop performance since she'd walked in the door. But I didn't. Instead, I grew even more annoyed, until eventually I wasn't saying anything, not even to Helen. That's when Bobby brought up the subject of coming out. Leave it to Bobby to pick my least favorite topic of public discussion.

Mostly, people's stories were funny. Carol described having had so many lovers during her marriage that when one of them turned out to be a woman, her husband felt that was the least of it. Then Pat told about going to a lesbian club, shortly after starting her first job at a department store, and running into, of all people, the woman with whom she split her shift in cosmetics. But it didn't work out because after that weekend, which happened to be Labor Day, whenever one was off the other was working. Helen, who had shocked all her friends in high school by declaring she was bisexual, finally slept with a woman in her late twenties.

"We took Quaaludes," Helen said. "Honestly, when you're in that kind of shape, you're not even picky about what *species* you're having sex with."

Marge had the most romantic story. She described meeting her first female lover at Burt's day camp in Westchester, where both were counselors...Marge the drama instructor and her friend the art teacher. After camp was over that fall, they spent every day in bed together while their husbands were at work, then got up at three and did the housework until their children returned from school. Later, each would make dinner for her respective family, then go off to rehearsals at the aforementioned community playhouse, where they'd stay late to make love. For a moment, I had a horrible thought that this first lover was Bobby...but when a moment later she took her turn, I realized she couldn't have been.

Bobby cut right to the chase, informing us that the spring of her freshman year, a guard at the women's college she attended found her after curfew in the parking lot, half-naked with a date, in a red Ferrari. She described the ensuing furor with which her housemother, next the dean, and then the president of the college had greeted the news, the next morning, that the other party had been a woman.

"It was uproarious," Bobby said. You knew this was a lie,

simply from her language. That same day, Bobby was expelled, and having been disowned by her family, lived for the next decade with the driver, a woman much older than herself, who it turned out had a problem staying sober. To top it all off, the red Ferrari had been borrowed.

"So much for truth in advertising. So much for college," Bobby said. If I hadn't disliked her so much, I would have felt sorry for her. "And you?" she turned to Burt. I had the impression Bobby was afraid to slow down, that if she did she might be overtaken by that woman in the car.

"It was easy for me," Burt said. "My mother was a lesbian…I had dates with boys." He shrugged, and everyone nodded, though I couldn't imagine what it must have been like not to be totally divided against yourself and your own desire at that age.

I was the only one who hadn't spoken, and Bobby, sitting directly across the table, started pushing me. I told them I'd come out at boarding school, but that I didn't want to talk about it.

"You don't want to talk about it?" Pat repeated, raising her eyebrows to look at Bobby.

"It's none of your business," I made my point more obvious. People got up and began clearing the table.

About a half hour later, Burt, Helen, and I left…ostensibly because we had to get up early. But the truth was, none of us could stand being with Pat and Bobby any longer. Marge and Carol might like them for old times' sake, but in our case, that didn't apply, nor would it ever. In the elevator, we compared notes on their transgressions.

"*You don't want to talk about it?*" I mimicked Pat.

"An older woman in a red Ferrari…sure," Helen said. "I'm surprised she didn't claim it was Tallulah Bankhead."

Then Burt began tap dancing, recreating Bobby's outsize gestures from the living room. We laughed so hard that Burt had to stop and catch his breath, leaning against the railing at the back. Suddenly, the elevator door opened on a random floor, terrifying all of us, because that's the way the man had trapped the tenant. But no one was there, thank God, and we descended, without mishap, to the lobby.

It was outside Westbeth, a moment later, that we ran into Ramon. I wasn't surprised to see him, the way you never are with people you've been thinking about, though that's irrational. Besides, this was his neighborhood now. I realized he must have lost at least forty pounds, from crack, since I'd seen him a month before.

"Oh, Ramon," I said. "How can you be doing this to yourself?"

"Easy," was his reply. His eyes were socketed like a racoon's.

"You know, you were doing so well in school. You've read so many books...you know so much," I said, as if that could mean anything to him in his current state. I wanted to take his arm, but didn't dare touch him. Helen and Burt just watched. I'm not sure they understood what was happening.

"I know too much," Ramon said. He was always smart like that. But sometimes being smart is no use to people. There's some deeper place they're making their decisions, where a Montague will love a Capulet...where I myself had wanted one particular girl of all my classmates at boarding school.

All the leaves were orange, that October, while the expanse of grass behind Webster House had been bleached of color, like hay. We'd just played a field hockey game, and were still in our uniforms...pleated tunics with sashes, gym cleats, shin guards...walking up the asphalt path beside the infirmary. I fell behind, overcome by the beautiful fall weather. But it was also a season of the mind, in which I'd lived by myself for quite some time. The team ahead of me looked all legs in their short skirts, hockey sticks trailing, as they walked in the direction of the locker room. That's the age at which girls haven't yet settled into their bodies, before waists thicken and features become more pronounced.

Suddenly, I heard shouting, and a band of five girls came

running out of the classroom building into the quad fronting the newer arts and sciences complex. Its two-story wall of glass, through which you could see the chemistry lab on the first floor and the art studio above, rose like a window on other lives. Like a building I once saw being demolished, in Boston, where inexplicably people's towels still hung in the bathrooms, knickknacks occupied their shelves. It was as if at any moment someone might walk in from another room.

That's exactly how I felt, again, seeing Susan Feld cross the threshold of the art studio. She seemed to me, in that moment, not really good-looking...she was never that to me, with her straight sandy blonde hair and too skinny body, a type I would not be attracted to later...but expected, somehow, and longed for, unlike the other girls. I went into the building and climbed the stairs. Why? someone might ask. First, because like Burt, who years ago kept dreaming that he was dancing, I'd imagined kissing her every night. And also, because like Burt dancing now, desiring her was like some memory of my body from an earlier time, which I can only imagine to be childhood.

It says something about my personality that I chose to kiss her for real in front of a two-story glass wall, meaning that I've always needed to be exactly who I am...though at the time no one was walking by, I know because I made sure. I may be expressive but I'm not stupid. Nevertheless, it was all over campus by the next day. I think this falls under Helen's favorite topic of "Betrayal," not to mention "Hubris" on my own part, and possibly even "Power Corrupts" on Susan Feld's. Let's just say that homophobia and self-hatred in our daily lives are things I learned about, without once having to attend a meeting.

The way sometimes ruin becomes people, Ramon looked handsome as he stood before us. There was something essential about his humanness, I'll put it...all the extras burned away...like someone in an elevator with a madman, in this case *himself*. I reached for his hand, when, suddenly, he turned and ran toward the river. Ramon was a boy, I reflected then, who knew all the vegetables and all the animals...not to mention the countries and planets. There was also the matter of the books he'd read, his education far better than his peers'. Somehow I'd expected this knowledge to save him, the way once some paintings had saved me.

Higher Powers

Meanwhile, Alex had been trying to get pregnant. But with the work schedule both she and Rosalie had, as doctors, you wondered how they could fit in dinner with us, let alone have a child. Walking to their apartment a few nights before Christmas, Helen and I passed the fire station, where they had up a sign asking for donations of canned goods. Because it was way below freezing, there were hardly any homeless outside and the level of general street action was curtailed. That night, it was a kind of cold that makes light seem almost three-dimensional, the air around street lamps and store fronts taking on the look of transparent architecture.

We entered the lobby of Rosalie and Alex's building, on Sixth Avenue, then took the elevator up. After Rosalie opened the apartment door, we found Alex lying on the floor of the kitchen, with some cushions under her behind, both legs straight up against a counter. She said the donor had been there, a half hour before and they'd just done the artificial insemination.

Helen and I kissed Rosalie hello, and waved at Alex on the floor. Then we sat down at the kitchen table. I said we should probably do some kind of ritual to ensure fertilization, and while in one way I was kidding, in another way I wasn't. I figured it couldn't hurt, because Alex, like a lot of other women we knew, had been finding it impossible to conceive. I mentioned our friend Celia, who as a high priestess of feminism performed rituals for every occasion...birthdays, menopause, the summer solstice. But Alexandra didn't want to do anything that smacked of superstition.

"Do you mean to tell me," Rosalie asked Alex, "that you think we know everything about the human mind and how it interacts with nature?"

"No," said Alex. But you knew that as a scientist, that's exactly what she meant.

Helen told about someone she'd seen on Johnny Carson, who claimed to have bent a spoon just by looking at it...and also some people she knew who'd spent years chanting for peace in Vietnam. Rosalie reported a guru in New Mexico who told his followers to end world hunger by picturing their favorite foods.

"If people are so worried about starvation, they should send money to Ethiopia," Alex declared, "or go work in a soup kitchen." Just that week, Helen and I had bought tickets to a New Year's benefit for the Food Fund, which provided meals for the destitute in New York.

By this time we were in need of food ourselves, so Rosalie unwrapped the fish. Alex got up off the floor, but immediately moved to the couch, where her posture remained horizontal.

"It's like all these people are still living in childhood," I said, "when you actually believe you can make things happen just by wanting them to."

"We have now gotten onto the famous topic of wish fulfillment," said Rosalie. "But any of these belief systems is better than escape into drugs or alcohol," she added, pouring some oil in a skillet. "People have to have *some* theory about the nature of existence...in order to organize what happens to them."

I said I thought at least traditional religion had had its day. But Helen reminded me of the entire world of Islam, not to mention fundamentalist Christianity...as well as the time, one intersession, when the two of us were flying back from

Brussels on the now defunct People's Express and had witnessed some Hasidim, at sunset, trying to form a minion. One person short, they finally found someone among the passengers, a British subject who, wearing blond dreadlocks and a T-shirt that said *Fuck the Queen*, resembled the pop star Boy George. It shows how desperate they were that they threw a tallis over his shoulders and ran with him to the back of the plane. The funny part was, he knew all the Hebrew prayers.

"I'm not saying that religion is over," I told Helen, across from me at the kitchen table, "or that there aren't people left who still practice in traditional ways. But most people think of a higher power in a different, more contemporary, way now. Half the people I know who believe in God got religion at AA."

Then I gave the example of the televangelist I'd seen on TV, taped live, on a lakeshore, in Israel. Wearing a Jewish prayer shawl, he was sitting next to a fax machine and holding a cellular telephone. I said I thought religion, like everything else now...news, reproduction, food...was inextricably linked to its technology.

"Intermittently, the preacher would talk in tongues," I told them. "It sounded like pig Latin. Then he'd receive a fax or make a phone call to Dallas, where his ministry was. He kept talking about going to Gethsemane. Plus he made a lot of quasi-general comments, such as, 'In Arkansas, protect your home. God can put a wall around the house.' By *can*, he meant, first send in a check. Actually, he had the most conviction with simple diagnoses and cures, like, 'I see arthritis... away arthritis!' Then he'd reach out to the camera and tell people to touch their TVs. He called this the electronic laying on of hands." By this time, Alex was nearly apoplectic.

"But where's the logic there?" she asked. "I mean, say you could cure someone just by touching them...which I sincerely doubt...how could that *possibly* work through a TV set?"

"Maybe it's like shock treatments...you have to stick your hand in the back," I suggested. Everyone found this funny but pretended not to.

That's when Helen mentioned meeting someone who

actually could cure people with her hands. I can't say I was surprised. Honestly, more things have happened to Helen than anyone I know.

Frankly, Alex was skeptical about the healer, and so was Rosalie. Being doctors, they couldn't help it. But when Helen continued the story of interviewing the woman for a documentary her women's video collective had made in the seventies, both of them started to look interested. Used to skeptics, the healer told each of the four videomakers to pick a chronic ailment that conventional medicine had been unable to cure, and she would treat it, at each of the three taping sessions they'd scheduled. One picked her menstrual cramps, another her premature arthritis, *pace* to the televangelist, and the other her speech impediment.

"I had a hive," Helen said, "that hadn't gone down for months, baffling doctors and even my Aunt Bea, who'd been a pharmacist's wife. My cure was the most dramatic," Helen went on, "because she only had to give me one treatment. Her hands were very warm, and then they got hot, like irons. Within five minutes, the hive had disappeared by three-quarters, then after another five minutes it was gone...forever." Helen said she still had the scar, which, obviously, I'd seen, though I never knew it had such a dramatic history.

After that, Alex asked if the woman had cured the other ailments, too.

"Everything but the speech impediment," Helen replied. Everyone pondered this.

"She should have gone into analysis," Rosalie said, after a moment. The rest of us nodded. We'd all spent years horizontal on a couch, and not in the service of getting pregnant.

"Still," Alexandra added, "the whole thing could have been the power of suggestion."

"But, Alex, what exactly do you think the power of suggestion *is*?" Rosalie asked. I thought this was a good point.

After dinner, we did end up doing a kind of ritual. We looked at picture postcards and other memorabilia of the Beatles that Alex and Rosalie had brought back from their trip, in November, to England. They'd been in Liverpool, of all places, for a psychiatric conference, where Rosalie had read a paper. Whenever they took a cab anywhere, the drivers would make detours, without asking, to places like Penny Lane, which the song had made a landmark, and Ringo Starr's mother's house, where she still lived. A club where they'd been the house band had been torn down but there was a bank now in its place that people looked at instead. And, honestly, what did the Beatles represent to everyone if not some force much greater than ourselves? It was a comment on both publicity and rock and roll, but also on the possibilities of life, that four working-class teenagers from a declining port city in 1960 could become the most famous people in the world.

Alexandra asked if it was true that John had had an affair with Brian Epstein, their manager, who was gay and later killed himself. The unauthorized biography had said so. But Helen, who working for the news always spoke as if she had some off-the-record source, and often did, said *no*. What John Lennon had once said, she clarified, was that of everyone he ever knew, he *loved* Brian Epstein best.

"So who's the donor?" Helen asked, as we got up from the table.

"I am," Rosalie answered. All of us laughed, but actually we'd had a discussion once about whether it might be scientifically possible, one day, to merge two eggs. Alex and Rosalie, who were most in a position to know, said maybe, though no doubt it would be declared illegal, like everything else women want to do without men.

"Frankly, who the donor is is a secret," Alexandra told us. "Since he isn't going to be involved in parenting, we thought it would just complicate things for people to know. He agrees."

"Well, what did you go for, brains or brawn?" I asked.

"Actually, we went for *both* brains and brawn," Rosalie said. "The donor's a dancer who was also a Rhodes Scholar." At first

I thought she was kidding. But when I saw Alex look at her, like she was about to commit murder, I realized that what Rosalie had told us was true.

"Boy, this kid is going to be dangerous," Helen commented.

"*If* I ever get pregnant," Alex reminded her.

The morning of the Food Fund benefit, I went to the cash machine near Helen's. You spend half your life in this city trying to get money, particularly during the holiday season. I took the last place in line behind, in order, two gay men who didn't know each other, one an African-American and one a WASP; another black man who was part of the staff at Stuyvesant Town, the middle-class housing project east of First Avenue; a Filippina woman who looked like she lived in that housing; and an elderly white lady with a Pat Nixon coat and an expression of similar despair. Last but not least was a swami, in flowing robes, some sort of ankle rags, a turban.

The first gay man, the short white one, leather jacket, small hoop earrings, who was standing at the single machine, cursed, then grabbed his card and swung through the door. He looked hardly solvent, and I assumed he'd run out of money. But next, the second gay man was up, and suddenly the machine started making a funny shuffling noise. Abruptly, its console flashed, UNABLE TO DISPENSE MONEY AT THIS TIME.

"It's out," somebody said, and with that we all turned and exited to the sidewalk.

"The closest other bank is on First Avenue," I told both the remaining gay man and the swami. Neither of them would have been dressed warmly enough for winter, the one in the aforementioned flowing robe and the other in a denim jacket over a T-shirt, except that we were experiencing an early January thaw. By that time the man in the worksuit, and both the Filippina woman and Pat Nixon, had walked off. So it was just the three of us, waiting to cross Fourteenth Street.

When we got to the second cash machine, in a savings bank, which was open on a Saturday, our line was no longer in its original order. In a spirit of fairness, everyone began to rearrange themselves, including the Fillipina woman, who, having stopped somewhere else, had arrived at the door just after us. But then someone pointed out that the electronic console looked dim, and it was also suspicious that there'd been no preexisting line.

Suddenly, the gay man, who by rights was first, turned and offered his place to the swami. Initially, the swami declined, but when the Fillipina woman and I concurred, he reconsidered. It's not that we were convinced his card would work in a broken machine, it's just that, considering the options, we figured a spiritualist was our best bet.

The swami walked up to the cash dispenser, but what's sometimes typical of people who live a cloistered life, he had no idea how to use it. He was modest, however, and not embarrassed to ask for help. First I got his card in right side up, then the gay man found the *Enter* button. After that, the swami pressed the amount and code number himself. Everyone waited. Then absolutely nothing happened. The swami tried a second time. But again, no money materialized. The funny part was, he seemed genuinely surprised.

I finished doing some errands, with the cash I had, then went back to Helen's. Though I still had my apartment on Sullivan Street, I was pretty much living with her by then. As I let myself in, I heard the shower running in the bathroom. This was an unheard of event on Helen's part, on a Saturday at 10:00 AM. She usually got up around one or two, on weekends, then stayed awake half the night. I stuck my head into the steam-filled room.

"What's up?" I said.

"Work called," she explained. "They need someone to take a feed from London, then edit a package on the New Year in England, for Sunday."

"So how late are you going to be?" I asked.

"Late," she said. "You better go to the benefit tonight without me."

"Well, I'm certainly not going by myself," I told her.

"Of course not," Helen answered. "Take someone with you."

"But who's going to be free on New Year's Day night on such short notice?" I said. "Just losers." But by then I'd gotten carried away.

Suddenly, the shower stopped and Helen opened the curtains. She pulled me to her, all wet, and kissed me. She was trying to make up for her unexpected desertion. I thought of how much better my life had been since I'd met her, how she had a way of making the smallest thing seem worthwhile, of conducting each day in ways that gave it a kind of correctness, a proportion that, before her, mine had lacked. Sometimes, at night, when I couldn't sleep, she'd describe places she'd been to…in intricate visual detail. It was like dreaming a beautiful dream together.

"I have an idea," Helen said, grabbing a towel. "Why not go with Sandy?" Sandy, who lived in our building, had been one of the organizers of the benefit, and had sold us the tickets in the first place. His dance company was doing one of the performances at the ten o'clock set. "He's fun," Helen added, "and low-key, and…"

"OK, OK, " I interrupted. "I'll call Sandy."

The benefit was in a loft on Canal Street. Sandy and I walked, because as a dancer, he liked getting exercise, and besides, the thaw had held into the evening. We went straight down Second Avenue, past such longtime haunts as the deli at Tenth Street; next Gem Spa, on St. Marks Place, specializing in magazines and egg creams; then, a few blocks down, the Universal Church. A sign outside read, *If you have addiction, insomnia, suicidal thoughts, constant headaches, have been a victim of santeria or witchcraft, come and receive complete freedom.* We decided they had a huge congregation.

We cut west on Houston Street, then continued downtown on Lafayette to Canal. Extremely light on his feet beside me, Sandy walked as if his small supple body were a featherweight. In his late forties, he was one of those men who never look their age. In spite of a bald spot and little sprigs of wrinkles at his eyes, he made you think of Peter Pan. Finally, we arrived at our destination, which, Sandy had neglected to tell me, was all the way across town, at the entrance to the Holland Tunnel. There was a crowd outside the three-story loft building because it turned out they hadn't opened the house yet for the ten o'clock show.

The benefit for the Food Fund was running around the clock. Every hour, there was a different group of performers, for which they'd sold another round of ten-dollar tickets. Actually, I thought this was an ingenious organizational principle for making money, though probably some of the sets wouldn't be well-attended because of the hour or the popularity and/or quality of the performers. Sandy calculated that if they filled the house of 150 seats for every hour of the twenty-four, which they wouldn't, the grand total would come to $36,000.

Clearly, this was not going to eradicate hunger, even in New York. But being in community was a way so many of us saw ourselves now. Going to Act Up demonstrations, volunteering at the gay high school, collecting money for a food fund—half our lives were taken up with what people used to call causes. It was the kind of thing we did, and had evolved into a form of social life, because if we didn't do something, it wouldn't get done.

About five minutes later, they opened the door, and everyone began filing up to the third floor. The stairs weren't in such good shape, with dips in the old wood, so it was slow going. When we got to the top, they were selling tickets at a cardtable, which meant the set hadn't sold out, either that or they were overbooking. A pair of gorgeous girls were distributing programs.

After Sandy and I sat down, a few rows back from the stage, off center near the firedoor, I looked at my program. The star attraction was a lesbian comedian that Helen had seen, that fall, on a cable special. That was the way they'd organized each hour, one well-known counterculture celebrity to pull in the numbers, and the other performers in the service of art and/or democracy. They listed, of course, Sandy's group "Dancing Fools," and I also recognized the name of a long-time performance artist who used to collaborate with John Cage sometimes and Joseph Beuys when he was alive. The other two artists were supposedly a poet and a musician. But it's not always clear what that means at a downtown event.

There were a lot of dancers on our side of the aisle, you could tell from the posture they took in their chairs and their combinations of leotards. Sandy, not surprisingly, knew several of them, and got up to say hello. The last time I'd been around so many dancers had been a few years before...at a coffee shop on Sixth Avenue, below a second-floor ballet studio...the booths and counters full of teenage ballerinas, graceful with their long necks and straight knotted hair, their upswept posture like lilies yet to open. But not spontaneous enough for my tastes, and too feminine. Also too alike...if it isn't ballet at that time in your life, it's Girl Scouts or riding or a softball team.

Three of them were sitting in the booth in front of me, around fifteen or sixteen, the age when you talk at full volume because you sense older people are interested, which they are, but almost never in your ideas. One of the three was describing her younger sister who, she said, and this was her exact language, *couldn't distinguish one thing from another...who thought the students were stars*. I thought she was talking about the sky. I realized, in due time, that she'd been referring to the film of a dance rehearsal that she'd seen with her family at the Carnegie...that the stars were Margot Fonteyn and Rudolf Nureyev, and the students from the Royal Ballet. But I'd pictured that younger sister, sitting at her bedroom window at night, looking up, all her words attached to the wrong objects.

There was no curtain on the makeshift stage they'd built at

the front of the loft, and no backstage. A dozen lights stood on poles against the rear wall. It didn't look big enough either for dancing or performance. The audience space wasn't that big either, with ten rows of about fifteen folding chairs. For this set, they'd put in some extras.

After Sandy returned, the director of the Food Fund called for the audience's attention and introduced herself as she walked up onstage. She was pretty, in a conventional sense. Dressed in pantyhose, pumps, and a suit, she looked freshly kidnapped from midtown. The forest of lights behind her went brighter for a moment, then dimmed. It turned out she was also the mistress of ceremonies.

The comedian was the first performer up. She delivered a rapid-fire monologue, with jokes about things like PMS, promising new materials for breast implants, tampax on blind dates. You understand, this was a lesbian comedian, so we were hearing the kind of remarks you're not used to hearing in front of a mixed audience of 150 people even on Canal Street. Sandy, who has a prudish streak, just sat there looking straight ahead. I wondered what the director of the Food Fund thought, as she watched from the front row. When the comedian left the stage, grand as Mae West, whose topic was also sex, almost everyone applauded and whistled wildly.

This humor was some consolation when, after that, we sat through the poet. It became clear that she wasn't published when she arrived on stage with a thick black manuscript binder, and later I doubted that she ever would be. She took the idea of occasional poems to new extremes, documenting her and her mother's vacation to Hawaii, signing the lease on her first loft, seeing the actor Robert De Niro in a bar. The musician, right after her, played an instrument he'd invented himself...an amplified milk carton with viola strings. Even Sandy, who's artistically open-minded, started nodding off. It was the kind of musical performance I remembered from years ago...arrhythmic, atonal, and short on notes.

By then, thirty-five minutes had passed. But because of the

last two performers, it had seemed endless, like a dream that covers years. I was just about ready to cancel my membership in the avant-garde, and honestly, if I hadn't been with Sandy, whose company had yet to dance, I would have left. All I'll say is it's a good thing I didn't.

The woman who followed the musician was in her fifties, and one of the pioneer performance artists...before most people even knew what performance was...first coming out of the Fluxus movement, then doing all the early feminist stuff, like breaking dishes and pouring menstrual blood, later nudity and body work. Well known in Europe, but never above Fourteenth Street, she was a working artist who'd spent thirty years perfecting her craft, and when she walked up out of a seat in the audience onto the stage, people applauded. Her body, in a leotard, though of a different physicality from someone youthful...with more pendulous breasts, heavier thighs, an enforced stateliness...was nevertheless beautiful. I think that's where the thirty years showed most...in a startling compression of movement she had, like Sisyphus pushing boulders up a hill.

What she did next might have seemed ridiculous in someone else's execution. But not in hers. She started pulling strips of bed sheets from under the lip of the stage, the white tips of which must have been visible all along, though I hadn't seen them. Then she tied the ends to various of the iron light poles, and pulled them taut in her hands, wrapping them once around her palms, like reins. She might have been training a horse. Or weaving. Ariadne spinning thread through the labyrinth. When finally she let go of all but the longest strip, then wrapped herself up in it, all the time drawing closer to the pole, it made me think of the swami's turban. I thought about how all the world is like that...everything overlapping, the same things coming in many forms, different things coming in the same form...a transparency, an architecture of the mind.

Next, she began unwrapping herself by spinning in the

opposite direction, until the cloth was fully unfurled, then pulled taut. Stepping offstage, she simply let it go. As the end touched the floor, the lights went out. Again, there was whistling and applause. In fact, that would have been enough to redeem my faith in art, for the foreseeable future. But even that performance was nothing on what came next.

Three people immediately entered stage left, which meant via the staircase since there were no wings. They were an unusual trio as they stood there, a rather handsome stocky man in his thirties, an oddly blank-faced girl, maybe twenty, and a robust older woman whose age seemed indeterminate though I suspected she was actually quite elderly. Though they all wore tights, the last thing they looked like was a dance trio. But that was the way the "Dancing Fools" always worked, laying bare the nature of their craft in ways you wouldn't expect. Sometimes they didn't even dance.

The beginning of this piece was no exception. At first the three of them just stood there, looking around, then the man shinnied up one of the light poles and back down. He did it again, with difficulty. In almost any art form, this kind of primitivism wasn't for me, and I was starting to lose interest. But suddenly the older woman began to talk, at first to the other two dancers, then she turned downstage and began addressing herself to the audience. Her topic, though she spoke exclusively about her own past, was the history of modern dance.

She said that as a child, she'd been kissed by the Russian ballerina Anna Pavlova, which abruptly and unexpectedly changed her life. Later, in 1908, she attended Isadora Duncan's triumphant return from Europe to New York, which changed the direction of that life, to modernism. What went on onstage was one thing, she told us, but when women from the audience began to run up the aisles, shedding their corsets and jewelry, that was another.

"Don't imagine me," she instructed us next. Her upper body swooped in a small circle. "Imagine Isadora, her shoulders draped with scarves. Picture now, not these old bones bending, but see me down on the floor and rebounding." Then the woman started dancing, as a kind of afterthought, moving her limbs the way someone else might hum a tune. Behind her, the other two dancers began to take small, tentative steps. The way they moved, in tandem, seemed strange and unusual.

The woman said she'd become a Graham dancer. She described how the company brought both social themes and classical subjects into the world of dance: for instance, the portrayal of the poor in breadlines, along with such characterizations as the mythological Phaedra, who lusted for her stepson. She said that modern dance was about women discovering themselves and one another.

"Martha Graham taught me how to make a pot roast and be an adult," the old dancer told us. "We were pioneers," she said. "We stood for an hour, then moved."

That was the end of her monologue, and for a moment people remained silent. But then the applause started, and it lasted for some time. Later, I wasn't sure whether this had been a true story, or a performance whose intention was verisimilitude. Not that it mattered.

Finally, the audience quieted down. That's when the three dancers started moving again, together. There was a certain awkwardness to the choreography, I thought, which consisted of the three of them never letting go each other's hands, like Ring-Around-the-Rosie or some other child's game, as they swung around the makeshift stage. Looking at the iron light posts, like a grove of trees behind them, I suddenly thought of *Oedipus at Colonus*, a play I'd taught for years. That's when I realized, the way information comes at you sideways sometimes, that the girl onstage was blind. Suddenly, it seemed so obvious.

After that, each performed a short solo...first the Graham dancer, a kind of expressionist reenactment of the history she'd narrated, impersonating the heroines of dance...then the blind girl, who, twirling like a parasol, stepped perilously close to the stage's edge, but never over, as if attached to one of the cloth strips that earlier had divided the air. Next the man took his turn. He wasn't a natural dancer, with a kind of slowness about him, a lack of facility of movement, as if his body were some coat he'd thrown on against the weather. But as usual in life, what should have been his undoing was the very aspect of his dancing that dazzled.

"That's my friend Bob Remick, who I want you to meet afterwards," Sandy leaned over to tell me. "He was a Rhodes Scholar and was going on to a brilliant career as a historian. But he gave it all up to dance." I realized I'd heard this story before.

Just then Bob Remick reached out...he looked like a man underwater, towing his arms against the pressure...before the three of them re-formed their original pattern and danced a little longer.

"Well, he was right to do it," I said. This was a comment neither about raw talent nor rewards in any worldly sense. I just thought it suited him to be up there holding hands with an octogenarian and a blind girl.

Later, Helen and I lay in bed, telling each other what had happened that day. As usual, it was taking us some time to get through, particularly the Bob Remick part. Then, around midnight, who should call but the two doctors, which would have been ironic except that that *always* happens. Needless to say, I didn't tell them I'd just met their donor.

"Well, here's the news," Rosalie said. "Alex got pregnant the night you came over."

"Alex is pregnant," I told Helen, then said back into the receiver, "How wonderful! Congratulations! What?" I asked Helen, who repeated what she'd just said, and I repeated it for Rosalie, who told it to Alex.

"Helen wants to know if you think the ritual with the Beatles postcards did it," I heard Rosalie say. "Yes," she answered back to us, "only now Alex is afraid we'll have a boy. She thinks maybe we should have concentrated on a girl group instead."

"Well, you'll find out soon enough," I said. But I thought they could do a lot worse than having a miniature Dancing Fool around the house.

Soon, we hung up and turned out the lights. But I was wide awake because so much had happened...not to mention that I felt like Sherlock Holmes, having uncovered the identity of the donor. To help me sleep, Helen performed her usual trick. She started describing some of the video she'd used, that day, for her piece on the New Year in England.

First, she told me about Harrod's, the department store... how it looked from the street, and on the first floor, all the different kinds of merchandise and colors. Then she moved on to Westminster Abbey, inside and out...also Big Ben and Buckingham Palace, with those guards in the hats who won't smile. Helen continued talking, describing sheep farms and factories and pubs...Mt. Snowdon, Liverpool, the Straits of Dover. She spoke more softly now, creating images so clear I could see them. I wondered if anyone ever did that for the blind girl.

Suddenly, I thought of the first time I went to bed with Helen. At the time, I was like one of those afflicted congregants at the Universal Church...in need of complete freedom. Shedding my clothes, I must have felt like those women running up the aisles to Isadora Duncan, only instead of taking off jewels, it was more like putting them on. Everyone has those moments when someone unexpectedly invites you to *live*...like John Lennon loving Brian Epstein best, or Anna Pavlova's kiss.

The tape ended with some footage of the royals. When Helen said this, I remembered that Boy George look-alike, in his *Fuck the Queen* T-shirt, with the Hasidim. It struck me then that people form minions all the time, though not in precise numbers. I pictured Bob Remick with the Dancing

Fools...then with Rosalie, Alex, and the baby-to-be. That swami with the rest of us at the bank. Next, I thought of all four Beatles, with their listeners in Britain, then beyond. People are related in ways we can't begin to understand and ways we can...like if the homeless are hungry, you can collect $36,000 and feed some of them. You can teach someone to make a pot roast and dance.

Zen Project

Since the Guardian Angels had left, Helen's block had become so bad again that one night in March we'd had to call the police to escort us home. The half-dozen crack addicts that had congregated on our stoop, and the one next door, left when the police van made its first circle. But when the cops came by on their second sweep, just as we were about to climb the stairs, I noticed someone below. When Helen asked if it was one of the junkies, the officer who'd gone to investigate shouted up that *no*, it was only a psychopath. Then Helen and I leaned over the concrete side to see a man with a plastic bag for a hat, swinging a pop-top on a string.

This was funny, but the murder, that same week, of a cab driver on the corner of First Avenue was not. Neither was the fact that the front door didn't shut properly and the light in the foyer had been out for several days, in spite of our calls to the management company. It was an invitation to trouble-makers, a number of whom had accepted, pushing through the lobby into the building at all hours of the day and night.

It was a Tuesday night, later on in the month, that Helen and I were taking a cab home late. We saw a suspicious-looking character, in a long down coat, standing on the stoop of her building. Actually, his hood was pulled up over his head, so you couldn't see his face too well. But when I took another look, from the cab, I thought the person seemed familiar somehow, and he kept staring at us like we were familiar, too. Well, the truth was, we *did* know him, which we realized when he bared his head. It was Ricardo, who was waiting for Sandy, as he sometimes did late at night. Helen said men have the most peculiar relationships, and though I did think Sandy could give him a key if he was out late dancing, or even plan to meet him during the day sometimes, I figured it was an arrangement, like any other.

It broke our hearts, how lovely Ricardo was, when we greeted him on the stoop. So apologetic about scaring us, as he stood there in his down coat, which he was proud of, because he'd just gotten it, on sale, at the end of the season. He declined our offer to wait in the lobby, saying the coat made it seem like summer outside. Then Ricardo mumbled something about water flying out of a window above, and sure enough, the steps were covered with puddles. We told him the problem was that no one had recognized him in the hood, which was true. But it was also his unmistakable style—young and Puerto Rican.

Helen and I felt terrible as we walked toward her apartment in the back. As she pulled out her keys, we looked up to see Seymour, a new tenant, coming down the stairs. It turned out he was the one who'd dumped the water, and having seen us come in from his window, wanted to find out about the man in the hood. When we told him it was only Ricardo, who knew Sandy and wouldn't hurt a fly, Seymour felt even more terrible than we did. He said he hoped that current social problems hadn't turned him into a vigilante.

By Friday, things had returned to normal, if you want to call it that. I myself had changed the bulb in the lobby and Seymour had improved, though not successfully repaired, the front lock. We'd scheduled a tenants meeting for Sunday, to discuss the situation in the building, and on the block.

That evening, we were going to have dinner with Helen's

longtime friend Miranda. Before we left, we found a bottle of wine, and some mugs to take as a housewarming present, because the last time we'd seen Miranda at home had been in the loft on lower Broadway. She and her husband Tor had shared it with the designer Tanya T., before the three of them got thrown out when the building changed hands. The apartment where the two of them had ended up was on Rivington Street. Once the drug capital of the Lower East Side, that block now shared its title with a lot of others, including our own.

Though it would have been only a short walk downtown, we were late, so we took the car. Luckily, there was a parking space right in front of the building. After we locked up, we pressed Miranda's buzzer, then pushed through two doors into a small renovated lobby. We walked past a row of brass mailboxes, equally new, to the back, where we began climbing the stairs, a distinctly old-fashioned feature.

Miranda met us on the fourth floor, at the door of her new apartment. She was wearing tights under a T-shirt that said, "Say cheese!," which I thought could be her philosophy of life. Most people would have been suicidal, losing five thousand square feet, which you would never have again in this lifetime. But they'd made the best of it...ending their lease with a huge party, to which everyone they knew was invited. Still, that party had marked the end of an era, because Tanya had started her design studio there, and Tor's band, which was doing well now, had first rehearsed there, and he and Miranda had gotten married in that loft, in 1980.

Even though we were forty-five minutes late, Helen and I were the first to arrive. So Miranda took us on a tour of the apartment. First, she showed us the bathroom, looking like some rocketship interior, with its dropped ceiling and complicated panel of knobs for the heatlamp. Then, on either side of the hall, further down, two alcoves that had been intended as offices. But while Tor's had remained one, sleek-looking in chrome and leather, Miranda's had more recently become her dressing room. Here an ornate bureau took up most of the tiny space. A mirror propped above it was capped on one side by a straw hat decorated with cloth crimson roses. You could smell perfume in the air, and Helen said it was like walking into the nineteenth century.

Back in the foyer, we looked at the storage cabinets a carpenter had built. We admired the molding and baseboards, which it turned out Tor and Miranda had done themselves. Helen said that we should probably spend some time fixing up our own apartments, but that neither of us knew how. Miranda shrugged and said you had to be into it, which I realized was her modest way of referring to Tor's handiness. She was basically the helper, she explained, handing him nails and pieces of wood, then stepping back before he hammered to see if everything was straight. Some other woman saying the same thing would have sounded hopelessly sexist...but the way Miranda put it made it seem random that Tor had received certain talents and she others.

At the end of the short front hall, we stepped into a space that had once been several rooms, tenement style, but now, without walls, held the rest of Tor and Miranda's possessions. Hat tree, dining room table with chairs, three sofas and a coffee table, record collection, sound system, Tor's backup amplifiers, coats and dresses on a clothes rack in the corner behind a double bed...everything was visible at a glance. The apartment was small compared to the loft...anything would have been...but it was nice, and along the front a half-dozen windows faced east, into the street. You could see for quite some distance, across a parking lot then a schoolyard, almost to the river, where the projects at Avenue D blocked the view.

As we followed Miranda between the dining set and the edge of the white chenille bedspread, you could see tape on the floor where the bedroom would be. Tape also marked the space for a closet and the entryway between the kitchen and dining room. Miranda said they were going to have to get a permit for the work, even though they owned the apartment, and even though before the developers' renovation, the space had probably had the same number of walls as they intended to build.

The kitchen was on the other side of a piece of tape that, in spite of myself, I had trouble crossing. Amidst the new appliances, which had been hidden by a half-wall that backed the refrigerator, Miranda began stirring something on the stove. Helen admired three doors, two leaning against the wall, fully stripped of paint, and another, in progress, that was laid across saw horses. Doubling as a table, it held plates of hors d'oeuvres and a stack of cookbooks, along with the stuff you find in any home...hair ribbons, a flashlight, some sunglasses, loose change, a box of film. Miranda said that stripping the doors had been her Zen project since they moved in. When I asked exactly when that was, Miranda said almost three years before, and none of us could believe it.

The last time we'd seen Miranda really to talk to, it took us a moment to figure out, had been at Victor's fortieth birthday party. At the time, Helen had never met Victor, who was my friend, though when she finally did, she thought he looked familiar. I'd dragged her to his party, where we thought we wouldn't know anybody but Sydney, my ex, who Helen was not exactly dying to spend the evening with. But then five minutes after we walked in, Miranda and Tor arrived. That's when Helen remembered, the way a dream comes back to you, at a particular cue, that the reason Victor looked so familiar was that she'd seen him over the years at Miranda's parties.

Victor's party was entirely different from the one that had closed the loft, the latter full of avant-garde musicians and a number of men in skirts, which was a design craze that year, not to mention all the young women with video cameras, from Miranda's production class. At the birthday, held in Victor's friend James's tastefully decorated apartment, overlooking the Hudson, uptown, a trio of African-American musicians, the only black people there, had played Cole Porter songs. The other guests looked rich, though they might not have been. A famous actor sat off in a corner of the living room, among friends, including Sydney.

I remember a woman I'd met years before in a bar and nearly went home with, dancing all night by herself. I danced with her again, for old times' sake, though she couldn't quite place me. Later, I spent time with Victor's and my lawyer, Kay, whose office was also home to a family of finches. When you went there, they hovered like ideas around your head. Meanwhile, Helen and Miranda caught up, while Tor talked with the trio about music on their breaks.

The dining room table at Rivington Street was set with several places, and I asked Miranda who else was coming. She said Tanya, whom I knew about, and also Victor and Ed Moss. The two of them had been an item for five months now. When, at some point, I'd asked Victor if he was in love, his answer betrayed the marshy ground of human relations. *Let's put it this way*, he replied. *I'm having functional sex with a man I've met more than once.*

After that, Miranda mentioned the first names of three other men who I was assured by both her and Helen that I'd met before. But I knew that if I had met them, it had to have been at one of those parties in the loft, where you couldn't talk to anybody because the music was so loud, or at some Act Up event, and I was sure I wouldn't remember them. Miranda said that she'd known two of these men since art school in Florida, of all places, and that the day after graduation all three had bought plane tickets to New York. Here, one of her friends had met and fallen in love with the third man, with whom he still lived. It was a truly romantic story. Helen said that one was a photographer for Seventh Avenue, and that the other two were stylists. Three themes had emerged from the guest list that evening: homosexuality, fashion, old friends. It turned out that Tor, whom I'd been expecting to walk through the apartment door any minute, was on the road for eight weeks with his band.

A little after eight-thirty, everyone else arrived, and at once.

The first person to make it up the stairs was Teddy, whom I recognized immediately. With his noble face and close-cropped gold hair, he'd always reminded me of the way I'd pictured Julius Caesar. When Helen asked if he remembered me, Teddy addressed me by name without help. He was the kind of person who looked you in the eye when he spoke and listened carefully to what you said back. He had a kind of seriousness that wasn't oppressive but uplifting…as if he intended to keep track of things that other people let slide.

Teddy was accompanied by Keith, whom I hadn't met, and who I assumed was the boyfriend fallen in love with years ago. He was shorter than Teddy, and stockier, with a thatch of brown hair that made him seem still boyish though he had to be well into his thirties. There was a wholesomeness about him, which seemed to belie his leading role in Teddy's romance, though the truth about sexual taste is there's no accounting for it.

About a minute later, Victor emerged from the hall, his shoulder-length hair pulled back. He had that startled look on his face that I noticed from the very first time I met him, as if life were some kind of ongoing surprise, which it is. Victor was wearing his usual leather jacket and blue jeans, but with a fancy embroidered shirt that lent his outfit an odd but convincing formality. I'd seen Ed earlier that week at the high school. In a pair of dress slacks and a turtleneck, his hair in a crewcut, he looked incongruous next to Victor even now.

Julian, whose boyfriend was in Milwaukee for a sister's wedding, Miranda told us, buzzed right after that, and it turned out that I remembered him, too. You never would have guessed he was in fashion from the unironed shirt he wore over baggy corduroy pants…or maybe that was just the point, maybe you would. Julian waved a bunch of tickets for a fashion show in July, which he was organizing to benefit the Gay Men's Health Crisis.

As people kissed hello, it became clear how much they liked each other. You knew it had to do with having known one another so long, through so many periods of their lives. Next, Tanya T. arrived, in a silk sheath, which though it looked picked out at a thrift shop, I knew she'd designed herself. Her brown hair was twisted up, also in a style from the fifties, so that the impression she gave was one of complete and utter appropriation. I remembered Helen's goddaughter, B.J., once asking us if Tanya was the real Barbie.

Tanya was the last to join us in the living room area, as we sat down to drinks on the sofas and chairs around the coffee table. That night, we had a lot to talk about, because all of Eastern and Central Europe had recently gotten liberated from communism, not to mention the changes in the Soviet Union. Miranda announced that she was serving Polish mineral water and Russian vodka in honor of that sector of the world. Someone got onto the topic of democracy.

"Everyone says this is a victory for us. But it isn't," said Helen, from where she sat between Victor and me on one of the couches. "People overthrew their totalitarian governments not because of democracy, but so they could buy things...things they saw on TV."

"Democracy is over," Julian agreed. "Once it was a world-historical idea. Only now it's become synonymous with capitalism, so that people use that word when what they really mean is a free-market economy."

"Yes, but you're forgetting the social change of a democracy," Victor told him. "Certainly, the accumulation of both wealth and property has been one force that's driven American society. But we've also interpreted the Constitution to gain more freedoms for more people...first the vote, then access to other civil rights."

"Good luck when the Russians actually do get democracy," I said, "because then they can foul up their country the way we have ours." I was thinking of a woman I'd overheard in a coffee shop, who'd asked the man she was with if you had to *run* for Senator. "I used to have more faith in people," I confessed, "...in their judgement."

"It's true," Ed Moss added. "In three months they overthrew half the totalitarian governments behind the Iron Curtain, and here we can't even get people to vote." Everyone shook their heads.

There was a pause in the conversation while Teddy and Miranda went to get more hors d'oeuvres. Afterwards, we cheered ourselves up by listing all the grass roots movements that committed people had organized. Like Earth First! and the other environmentalist groups. The Pro-Choice movement and AIDS activism. But as we got to talking, we realized the extent to which reactionaries had gotten organized, too. There seemed to be so many fundamentalists, survivalists, Moonies, skinheads, LaRouche followers now...that we wondered if anyone was left who we used to think of as a normal citizen.

"About the only real mass movement in *this* country now is the anti-fur movement," Keith said. He told us about a ski resort in the Rockies where the city council had voted to ban wearing fur. Resting his hand on his boyfriend's leg, Teddy said it was actually *selling* fur that they'd banned, but that that was amazing enough. Keith looked annoyed.

"I think the anti-fur movement is about *class*," Victor said. "A backlash against the rich, or, at least, ostentation. Not that that in any way excludes the rich from joining in. Think of all the wealthy liberals who gave money to the Black Panther party in the sixties," he went on, "before the government tried systematically to assassinate its leaders in a series of shootouts. But most of those were bungled, so that later they had to come up with criminal charges...in Huey Newton's case, murder, and in Bobby Seale's, conspiracy, for his role in the demonstrations at the Democratic Convention in Chicago. I wasn't political then," Victor admitted, "but I remember."

"I think one of them, one of the black revolutionaries, recently became a clothes designer," Tanya added.

"Eldridge Cleaver." Helen sounded pained. "The man who wrote *Soul on Ice* in prison and later ran the Panthers' international headquarters in Algeria, after everyone else had renounced the party, started selling crotchless pants."

"With knitted codpieces," someone threw in.

"Well, at least he's tried to keep going in life," Miranda said. "There's nothing worse than those people who still walk around wearing bellbottoms and pachuli oil. I have a cousin who in 1975 announced that he was dropping out of society and, to this day, lives in Woodstock in a treehouse."

"In a treehouse?" Ed Moss repeated.

"Actually, it's not as bad as it sounds," Miranda told us. "Tor and I went up there for the weekend once, and they had rugs and a TV...even a heated towel rack. But there's something peculiar," she added, "about living twenty feet off the ground on a piece of plywood." People nodded.

"On the other hand, dropping out *is* a philosophically defensible position," Victor said. But Teddy, Helen, and Julian disagreed with him.

After that, we moved to the dining area, where everyone sat down and began eating. The table was nice, rectangular and made of oak, the kind you used to get cheap upstate, though now they cost hundreds of dollars. The place settings, Miranda told us, were things she'd picked up at an estate sale last summer. In fact, the gold-rimmed plates and silverware looked like they should have been in some formal dining room in Connecticut, rather than in a tenement without walls on Rivington Street. It occurred to me, that's what had been happening in the world, too...and in people's minds...all the categories breaking down. Only, the problem was, nobody knew what to put in their place...how to think about things now...not governments, not social movements, not ourselves.

Right before we left that night, Julian sold everyone tickets for the fashion show. It was one concrete thing we could do. I noticed, a few minutes later, as Victor descended the stairs before me, how stiff he was. When I asked him how he'd been feeling, he said fine. He'd just been working out too strenuously at the gym.

*

The tenants meeting, on Sunday, was at 8:00. I was expecting a lot of people to be there, but when Tom opened the door, the only one in the living room, besides him and Carolyn, was Brenda, who lived directly above us. Brenda was in her aging-starlet phase, having recently been murdered in a Francis Ford Copolla movie. Sitting at a cardtable near the entrance to the kitchen, she was wearing dark glasses and a long platinum wig. Standing behind her, Tom and Carolyn looked exactly like what they were, two freelance writers in their late thirties, who'd lived together for as long as anyone, and probably they, could remember.

After that, Jane, whose apartment was beside Helen's in the back, arrived. We all made jokes about only the hard-core, long-term tenants attending the meeting. This group knew each other pretty well, if only because, living in such proximity, we'd heard each other's fights, lovemaking, and changing taste in music over the years. Plus, we were all about the same age and generation of New Yorkers. First Helen then Jane signed a notepad on the cardtable, after which Tom offered everyone coffee. Pointing at the pad, Carolyn said she was going to keep the minutes.

A moment later, there was another knock. It was Seymour, the new tenant. Immediately, he and Helen and I began rehashing the incident with Ricardo and the water, which by this time had become quite funny. After that, the story had to be repeated for every person who came into the apartment. Over the next few minutes, we told it to Bob, who'd been in the building for twenty-five years; Frank, who used to be our manager but had retired because of aggravation; and Arthur and his boyfriend, Allen, both of whom arrived in suits from work. Next, Marsha breezed in, totally plastered. After the seats ran out, people stood or sat on the rug. At 8:20 we began the meeting.

Our initial conversation was fraught with complaints, comments, and suggestions. The complaints were: One, *secu-*

rity...meaning the door, which Tom, our host, demonstrated was still broken by going out into the hall then the lobby and pushing back through without his key...also the roof door, which the top-floor residents, represented by Allen and Arthur in 5A and Marsha in 5B, attested was falling off its hinges. Two, *billing problems*...which included incorrect MCI raises for the new boiler and windows, not to mention losing people's checks or cashing them without record, which was incompetence not grand larceny, everyone agreed, but amounted to the same thing. More *security*...which we went back to because we'd forgotten about the light bulbs, both in the lobby and in the alleys, most of which were burned out. This led to, three, *maintenance*...for example, replacing those bulbs...and adjusting the hot water, which alternately didn't exist or was so scalding you could burn your hand turning off the tap. Someone said that the theme of this meeting was "No one's minding the store," and Carolyn wrote it at the top of the minutes. People voted, with a show of hands, that we should try to dump the management company.

Then Tom, our host and representative on the block association, gave a report about the last meeting at our local precinct house. Basically, the cops had said there was nothing they could do about anything.

"You wouldn't believe those meetings," Tom told us. "Even the Hell's Angels come. But you know they're not there to get *help* from the police; they're there to check what the police are up to." I said I was glad some things stayed the same.

This led to a discussion of whether the block had been worse during crack or heroin. People who'd been pioneers on East Thirteenth Street...a few of them, like Bob, going back decades...recalled their experiences. Bob said that the heroin addicts used to score in Union Square, then wander east along Fourteenth Street. Marsha remembered ambulances pulling up to a coffee shop, on the corner there, at all hours of the day and night, to cart off the ODs. Being drunk, she repeated this.

Arthur added that though you weren't so regularly accosted going out then, people's apartments got robbed more frequently. The first year I knew Helen, her own apartment was burglarized. They came up the fire escape in the back, then in a window, which was gated and shuttered, so they just pulled out the frame with a crowbar.

After that we took a mental inventory of the apartments... who of the tenants was missing...and who could be counted on to sign a letter to the landlord. We started with the three sisters, whose task at their age, and on the fourth floor, was not to get to Moscow but down the stairs...the two new young women, also on that floor, one of whom had replaced the depressed call girl who'd tried to blow herself and the rest of us up by leaving the gas on, one night. Then Marsha counted Sandy, who lived at the top with her and Allen and Arthur, after which Jane remembered the Changs, whose teenage daughters were always making out with dates under the stairs. We predicted that most of these tenants would sign.

We moved on to the ancient history of the building. Something about going through all the apartments, as a kind of form, had acted as a springboard to the past. It was the rent-control tenants who knew the most, though Helen had lived above the laundromat further down the block before moving here, so she'd seen quite a bit herself. First, Arthur mentioned the woman across the street who thought she was being gassed through her floorboards...also the old couple, the Pizzaros, who'd lived up on top, next to him, before Sandy. The husband was a terrible drunk, who everyone remembered falling down the stairs. Marsha explained that the couple didn't have a phone and she'd always have to be the one to call 911. Bob said Mr. Pizzaro used to go up on the roof sometimes, when Mrs. Pizzaro wouldn't give him beer money, and curse any Puerto Ricans below. In turn, they'd urge him to jump.

Meanwhile, Seymour looked alarmed. I don't think he knew what he was getting himself into, moving to this building, on this block, in this era. Actually, it wasn't a life I'd been brought up to live myself. But who had been? Carolyn announced the end of the meeting, and people began to get up. Just then, Sandy stuck his head in the door, and Seymour, who was standing right next to him, began to apologize for the incident with Ricardo. Our friend got this look on his face, which I think was a cross between embarrassment and amusement.

"You know, Ricardo mentioned the water," Sandy said. "But he never said anyone *threw* it at him." We all howled with laughter.

"So what's this thing with the water?" Brenda turned to Seymour, coming right to the point. She adjusted her platinum wig.

"I used to live in Little Italy," he replied, "and all the old ladies would do that when there was trouble on the street. They'd just go up to the roof and dump some water. So I decided to try it myself."

"Well, you couldn't have known it was Ricardo," I said. "We thought he looked suspicious, too, with the hood," I added, for about the hundredth time that evening. But everybody just kept laughing, as if we were hearing the story for the first time, all over again.

That's when I thought of Miranda's Zen project, those three doors that, in the house of life, are always opening. And you have to step through them, whether you want to or not, into a new time and a new place. Everything changes, and probably for the worse, if Thirteenth Street was any indication. But as our friends had in losing their loft, you make the best of things. You throw a party and invite everyone you know.

Gay Pride

On Gay Pride Day, Helen and I walked over to Fifth Avenue to watch the parade. We'd made plans to meet Rosalie and Alex afterwards, either at two that afternoon on the steps of the Jefferson Library or, if we missed them there, later, at the Palladium. On an occasion when half the lesbians and gay men in New York State and beyond congregate in downtown Manhattan, Helen thought it was unlikely we'd find them anywhere. But I had a feeling we would...because that's the day you see half the people you ever knew, planned or not.

We got there early, for once, and though spectators jammed the sidewalks, the procession was still uptown. Policemen and -women, stationed at the curb, kept asking people to stay on one side of the avenue or the other. But even they knew it was a lost cause. Every few minutes, you'd hear a shout, before a pair of old friends, maybe lovers, recognized each other from opposite sidewalks. The whole scene looked like something out of a Hitchcock movie...as if everyone present were under a compulsion to run into the street and kiss.

It was sunny and hot, for June, and the crowd was in high spirits. Total strangers talked and laughed amongst themselves...a phenomenon you don't see so much anymore. Occasionally, someone would walk by encased from head to toe in black leather, despite the season...alternately in such scant attire as a jockstrap. There was an undercurrent of energy that comes from such exhibitionism in public, and the desire people always have, whether they admit it or not, to watch.

Though the parade was still several blocks away, you could hear the structure of the music, like a distant windchime. Eventually, Helen and I found a spot where we could see, under the awning of an apartment house near Eleventh Street. Our view here was unobstructed, except for one very tall man we figured we could move to the side of, and there was also a fire hydrant Helen could stand on to videotape. Across the street, the First Presbyterian Church took up the entire block, its nineteenth-century grandeur like some joke on the world that had followed.

Helen had finished loading a cassette into her camera. Having turned from the people around us, she was now taping the crowd across the street. Here, in front of the church, the kind of New Yorkers I remembered from an earlier era were filling paper cups with water on a cardtable. You could just imagine them on a freedom bus, twenty-five years before, wearing the same unassuming styles they did that afternoon...the men in short-sleeved shirts with belted trousers, and the women in patterned sheaths and flats. Gray hair ruled the day, though they weren't so much older than Helen and I were.

That's when I saw Monica. I grabbed her arm, and pulled her toward me from where she was passing near the curb. Helen, who'd met her twice before at parties but I could tell didn't remember, said hello before returning her camera to her shoulder. Monica told me that Rodger was back in Ohio, more wasted even than before, hanging on by a sheer force of will he'd used, for years, in his work.

As Monica touched my hands, I marvelled that our friendship had lasted. I thought of all the people gone by the wayside, who once upon a time I'd liked or even loved better than her. But you can't predict, based on any kind of conscious knowledge, who'll be left when you look back on a decade, or two, for that matter. And then something else happens...the people you've known so long mean more to you because of that fact.

I knew one reason the two of us had sustained such good will over the years was that we'd never slept together. Not that forbearance was my strong suit in those days. I went to bed with any number of girls I would have been better off remaining friends with. We all did. It's just that in my own case, it wasn't ever *beauty* that moved me.

We talked a little longer, catching up on the last year or so, which it hadn't been possible to do at Rodger's reception. For both of us, the end of our twenties had marked the end of a life in the theater, her as an actress, myself backstage. But while I'd gone on to a Ph.D. and teaching, because the plays themselves were what interested me finally, Monica had never been able to start over, at least not with that self that had wanted to act. For years she'd had jobs...like managing a boutique or modelling shoes...that she'd quit in anguish before accepting another. She was currently working for the Japanese.

As for love, Monica said she was with a woman much older than herself now, and I hoped that she'd found somebody nice, for a change. People think that being beautiful protects you. But I remembered Monica being left by most of her lovers, after a few months, sometimes a year, during the decade of our twenties, when we spent so much time together. With women, the same as with men, good looks tend to up the ante, and there's even more vitriol when someone doesn't turn out to be the fantasy. Because no one ever is, over time. Because, actually, the fantasy isn't about the other. It's about yourself.

Monica and I hugged good-bye. We swore we'd get together that summer, which I knew was unlikely, though both of us meant it, in our way. Then, amidst the shouts of police, my old friend crossed Fifth Avenue then disappeared.

Facing uptown now, Helen had been videotaping all this time. I think it was the angle of her shoulders, the way they expanded in the sunlight, that reminded me of how specific desire is. How a woman's back turned away from me, a total absorption in something other than myself, had always inspired love. I had to admit, I wasn't any smarter than Monica...just luckier...in the way my thirties had turned out.

By now the parade had reached Fourteenth Street, and the crowd around us began to clap. A familiar figure was at the front of the procession...with wig, gown of gauze, baton in hand...drawing figure eights across the avenue. Some people think it's a mistake, leading with a drag queen on roller skates, the one day we have the media's attention. But other people think it's a mistake to take a drag queen on roller skates literally. To me, it says something about being gay that each year this becomes an entirely serious debate, touching on such issues as the right to carry a magic wand.

I remembered back to when I myself got upset at all the marchers you'd just as soon straight people wouldn't see on TV. Like the S&M contingent, in same-sex pairs, one attached to the other by a leather collar on a chain, redundantly labelled *master* and *slave*. Or the man/boy love group, conspicuously lacking boys. Not to mention the women with beards. But now I don't feel that way. And as for the drag queens, who number in the thousands that day, never mind Rollerena, I think anybody who can march six miles in high heels deserves the coverage. It's what we've all had to do in our way.

Up close, Rollerena wore a pair of heavy-frame eyeglasses, giving a kind of intellectual spin to her outfit. She swooped near to take the hand of the very tall man in front of us, whom she'd sighted, like some beacon, from afar. After that, a gay and lesbian marching band advanced to fill the avenue. They were playing "My Way," one of a repertoire of double entendre songs you hear every year. Behind them, a handful of heterosexual politicians, who were doing their best to get into the spirit of things, walked with their ties unknotted, the women wearing purple sashes. Everyone waving.

A contingent of male and female priests marched next, in flowing pastel robes, blessing the crowd as they passed. Then, according to the truly strange specificity of that parade, and also its democratic order, there followed a phalanx of animal-lovers, holding or walking a surprising variety of pets. There were about two dozen dogs, as many cats, a ferret, two monkeys, and a llama. It looked like some misconstrued Noah's ark, in which the pairs were not of like species, nor opposite genders, but had been chosen solely on the basis of affection...one person and one pet.

After that, a caravan of cars, representing local merchants, drove by, covered with homemade decorations. The first was a red Volkswagen Beetle from one of the greenmarkets, transformed by a stem at the top to look like an apple, and driven by Koreans, who you weren't quite sure understood the context. The last and, I thought, most wonderful entry was from a lingerie store...a convertible, trailing crepe paper and balloons, on the top of whose backseat sat two women, engrossed in talk, while dressed in beautiful white lace slips. Unlike anything else that afternoon, it looked like a tableau from life.

People had been clapping continuously. The applause rose when a bunch of gay square dancers, sixteen men in groups of four, danced up, accompanied by a fiddler. In their cowboy chaps and Stetson hats, which you knew had been a selling point for recruitment, they looked like an all-male *Oklahoma!* This group was followed by a half-dozen women, dressed eclectically but each holding a large crystal that, according to a flyer they handed out, was recycling the crowd's energy for white witchcraft. Next came a soccer squad, who seemed indistinguishable from any other except for their pink shorts and silver tanktops. The players took turns bouncing a ball off their heads or insteps, never letting it touch the ground as they passed. The concentration of all three groups was riveting, as if not a thing in the world existed but the moment and their singular activities.

After a halt to let through the crosstown traffic, Jesse Jackson's Rainbow Coalition marched by in solidarity, then some of the St. Vincent's nurses, wearing street clothes. Next came the colleges, also on foot, a contingent that occupied several blocks. NYU, Barnard, and most of the other city schools were represented by quite a large group, even though classes were over for the year. The out-of-towners, including Harvard Medical School and Yale Law School, had a cluster of marchers each. Suddenly, I recognized two of my own students, holding hands, and oblivious, as if they were strolling in a forest. I called out to them. The girls waved madly, then went back to a kind of insistent talking that reminded me of the models in their slips.

Lesbian Mothers was next, their banner embroidered with flowers. Some of these twenty or so women were accompanied by children, while others held up signs referring to complicated custody battles. Most of the *Gay Fathers* walked with just a lover or friend, but one black and white couple, majestic as male models, pushed a baby in a stroller between them. *Parents of Gays* got the loudest applause, for painfully obvious reasons. There were three of them...someone's mother, who looked like an ex-mental patient, and an upright Episcopalian couple, who seemed unlikely candidates for any parade, let alone that one.

That's when the gay high school marched by, with Theresa carrying the banner. In sensible heels and a low-cut blouse, she led the way, followed by a contingent of boys wearing scarves and bikinis. Two girls, the only ones, took turns carrying a cardboard sign saying *Legalize RU486*. Ed Moss brought up the rear in his everyday receptionist's outfit...khakis, with a white shirt and tie. All morning, I'd been looking for Ramon, though the people from Outreach said he'd disappeared from the streets.

There was another halt to let through traffic, so people just marched in place for a while. A block uptown you could see the Mummers, in their strange shaggy uniforms looking like something you'd sight in the Himalayas. Suddenly, the lights changed, and the band started up again at full volume. As the middle-aged Philadelphians approached, in rows, a young biker beside us asked his boyfriend if they were gay. This is what Helen calls the "information gap." I told him the Mummers marched in most big parades and were, in every sense, independent and unaffiliated.

That's when someone with a sign that read *Come out of the closet and march* walked next to the wall of spectators, beckoning with what seemed to me like smug satisfaction.

"There goes the thought police," I said to Helen. I'd been in so many arguments over the last few years about who should come out publicly, and who didn't have to, that I was tired of the whole subject. I was also tired of people thinking they knew what other people should do.

I remembered Helen telling me a few years before about Artie, a producer she worked with, who decided to come out at work. After that, his preferred position in intercourse was speculated upon by the other men every time he left an edit room, and they took to engaging him in discussions about the sodomy laws or AIDS or the occasional homosexual murder. When the Crispo case broke, and the police found a leather mask containing the partially decomposed skull of a Swedish art student, beheaded during sex, a reporter actually asked Artie if he had any leads. Taking Artie as their warning, everyone who might have been considering otherwise, stayed in the closet. Helen said he used to be the most fun to work with of any of the producers, because he had a sense of joy about his work, an interest in every story. But the evening we met him for a drink, he looked like he was wearing goggles, and Helen said he'd gone on antidepressants. It's cruelty that wears people down.

The next group that meant something to me was a cluster of middle-aged people, three men and four women carrying two hand-lettered banners, made of sheets: *Matachine Society* and *Daughters of Bilitis*. The former started on college campuses in the fifties by young men wearing white shirts, ties and crewcuts...the latter by two women whose bulky likenesses I'd seen holding hands in an underground magazine when I was seventeen and in Cambridge on a day trip from boarding school. They were the first self-acknowledged lesbians I'd ever read about, and I remember wishing at the time that they were pretty, meaning I missed the point.

After that, the AIDS groups marched...with signs that bore acronyms of what had become an all too familiar language over the past years...Act Up, GMHC, PWA. Hundreds of men and dozens of women wore T-shirts printed with a variety of messages that nevertheless said the same thing: *Fighting for Our Lives*; *Still Alive*; *Kiss Me, I'm Positive*. They reminded me of that soccer squad with their ball in the air.

Several people in this group, clutching purple balloons, were handing their strings to the spectators. At 3:00 p.m., the procession was going to stop, when, after a minute of silence, the balloons would be released into the sky. What had started out as a quasi-political Mardi Gras, post-Stonewall, had turned, in recent years, into a memorial for the dead.

The parade got weirder. A float carrying both gay devil worshippers and gay tattoo artists crossed Twelfth Street. Next, an antireligion tableau, featuring three men dressed as caricatures of the Pope, Iran's Ayatollah, and Mary Baker Eddy, passed in the back of a pickup truck. Somebody's grandmother was being driven just behind in a mint-condition 1960 red Thunderbird convertible. Holding a sign lettered *God Bless My Gay Grandson*, she looked shell-shocked from all she had seen.

Her expression brought me back to the night years ago that Monica had brought her mother to a lesbian bar. To me this was unthinkable, a sort of crime, though against whom or what I wasn't sure, and I can still picture a small blonde woman, sitting at a corner table by the dance floor, prim in one of those drip-dry suits women wore for travelling then, her gaze unfocused so that she wouldn't have to look at the female couples slow-dancing within arm's reach. While Monica proceeded to get dead drunk then pick up the most masculine-looking woman in the bar, like some lumberjack in her flannel shirt and Frye boots, her hair so short even I was scandalized, I went to sit with her mother.

I remember, the way certain moments in life retain a kind of horrible clarity, that we discussed stained glass in Italy, where I had never been, and an agricultural method I'd read about, unique to Sri Lanka and Bali. Monica's mother was the kind of smalltown woman who prided herself on knowing about the world. At the time, I thought about how where we were must seem equally like another country, and in my own way I was trying to make her feel welcome. Around midnight, when Monica was nowhere to be found, I walked her mother home, through the West Village, to Monica's apartment. On the way, neither of us mentioned her daughter or what might have happened to her. Later, Monica said, in referring to the whole incident, *It was her or me*.

Meanwhile, the people at the church were still manning their cardtable. I think it was the exquisite politeness with which they offered the little cups of water that kept drawing my attention back to them. There was something touching about the way they served marcher after marcher at the curb, as if life were just one big tea party, to which everyone, everywhere, had been invited. I watched as a six-foot black man in a green satin dress curtsied, in thanks, to a middle-aged white matron. Even from across the street, you could see how flustered she was, before, rising to the occasion, she reached for his hand and kissed it.

"I hope you got that on tape," I told Helen, who had no idea what I was talking about. It occurred to me that, in her own way and in a different vocabulary, that's what Monica had wanted from her mother.

It was almost two, when we were supposed to meet Rosalie and Alex, and though several blocks of the parade were still to come, we left to find them. As Helen and I walked down a block, then west, the sidewalks grew more crowded. At Sixth

Avenue, we crossed with the light. Here you could see the parade filling Eighth Street, just below us. We recognized marchers who'd already passed, now making their way west to the pier. It was like a moment of *déjà vu*.

When we got to the Jefferson Library, whose architecture looks like something out of a Russian fairytale, Alexandra and Rosalie weren't there. But by this time, we were a half hour late.

"I told you we'd never find them," Helen said. "They were probably already here...or else they haven't gotten downtown yet. If they're near the end of the parade," she speculated, "there's no way they're going to make it for at least another hour, and by that time they'll assume we've gone on, even if we haven't."

"I can't think any of this through logically," I told her. "Let's just wait a while and see if they show up." So Helen sat down on the steps, while I got some sandwiches from a nearby deli.

"They're not coming," Helen said, glancing at her watch. It was now just before three, and I thought she was probably right. Hordes of people were pouring by on the sidewalk.

"Well, I guess we'll just meet them tonight, at the Palladium," I said, lifting Helen's camera.

"No doubt," she pronounced, in a tone that implied the opposite conclusion. We started walking west on Tenth Street.

"The Women's House of Detention used to be here...before they tore it down," Helen told me, pointing through the chain-link fence at a garden, which neighborhood people had grown in the lot beside the library.

"That's right," I said. "I'd forgotten. When exactly was that?"

"Till the mid-seventies," she answered. Helen reached into her shoulder bag and pulled out another two-hour cassette, which she proceeded to load into the camera on my shoulder.

"I don't know why anyone with a memory like yours is so

obsessed with documentation," I told her. We continued walking beside the fence, to the back of the lot.

"Prostitutes used to spend the night there after getting arrested, before being bailed out in the morning," Helen recounted. "In the summer, women would hang out the windows and talk to passersby."

"You're kidding," I said. Now you can't even open the windows in most buildings they build, let alone chat with strollers from a prison. Helen's description seemed more like a different reality than a different decade...the dispositions of the people sweeter, their customs quaint...like in some fairytale that library made you think of.

"I knew these people," she went on, "who got arrested for doing c.d. at the phone company. It was somehow linked with Dupont, the makers of napalm, during Vietnam. Anyway, the female demonstrators got sent to this prison and, once inside, decided to organize the inmates. At dinner, they told the prostitutes they were all political prisoners. That was true, of course," Helen said, stopping to admire a rosebush behind the chain links. "But, put that way, it wasn't useful information.

"They finally got somewhere when one of them brought up bringing in the ACLU to stop the routine strip searches and pelvic examinations. It was taken for granted that because the women were prostitutes, they didn't have the constitutional right to privacy."

When we got to the corner, Helen walked a few paces along the sidewalk then pointed into the sky over the garden. There was nothing to see, of course, just her memory of the torn-down building. The people passing next to us on the sidewalk looked up, until, finally, everyone on the block was searching the sky. People made funny remarks about who or what we might see: a gay UFO was the best. Suddenly, purple balloons began rising over buildings to the east, above the library and along Fifth Avenue. It made for an odd moment, as if time had happened backwards and all of us had been looking up in expectation of what later occurred.

I looked at my watch. It was three o'clock, a time to remember the dead. Each of us had a long list of our own already. I wondered when mine would include Rodger. Moreover, Victor had been losing weight recently, and some nights ran a fever they couldn't explain.

"I was walking by here once myself," Helen said, after the minute of silence was over, and people broke from their statuesque poses to keep walking west, "...after dinner at the Bagel Buffet with my sometimes girlfriend Nancy." Helen gestured across Sixth Avenue at one of the few remaining landmarks of a neighborhood she'd frequented for decades. "We were both poor, and that was our favorite restaurant. At any rate, I was walking right by here, one night, when this girl stuck her head out of a window on the top floor and began telling a very complicated story. I just remembered," Helen added, "because of all these people staring up. Actually, a crowd had gathered, but the story went on for so long, and then it became so fragmented, that everyone, including Nancy, lost interest and walked away. But I thought the girl was very creative," Helen said. "Probably also schizophrenic...or maybe she was just tripping."

"Well, what was the story about?" I asked.

"Herself...what else?" Helen answered. "Anyway, I stayed there and listened to the whole thing."

This didn't surprise me. Whenever Helen stayed up late, she never wanted to go to bed, and also whenever she was asleep, she hated to wake up. If she was at the movies, she wanted to go to another movie. Etc., etc.

"After it fell apart," Helen continued, "...I mean, the story didn't end, it just stopped...she started chanting, 'Free Joanne Swift. Free Joanne Swift.' Finally, I said something. I interrupted her and asked who Joanne Swift was."

"*She was*," I guessed. Helen nodded.

"So I just started chanting along with her. Not that I thought it would do any good, and I did feel kind of foolish there on the street by myself along with this girl, four flights up, in the Women's House of Detention. But in those days, you expected more unusual behavior from people in public, without the sense of menace we have today. People used to refer to themselves as *freaks* then, with a kind of pride...speed freaks, nature freaks, Grateful Dead freaks. I didn't want her to feel alone," Helen finished.

As we rounded the corner onto Christopher Street, we could hardly move in the crowd. It must have taken us a half hour to go three blocks. We were just approaching the intersection at Bleeker when I noticed a microwave truck from one of the TV stations parked in front of the army/navy store on the corner. Helen hadn't seen it yet, and I laid my hand on her forearm. When you work in TV news, you know all the camera crews, and, for good reasons, she wasn't out at work.

"Is that yours?" I asked. Helen followed to where I was looking and adjusted her glasses.

"I think so," she said. Then, as the crowd carried us closer, sure enough, the side of the truck said *News 4*. We were about to turn around and walk in the opposite direction, when suddenly the cab door opened and Nicholas jumped down. Helen started laughing and called out his name.

"I can't believe I got this assignment," Nick said, hugging us as we stepped from the stream of people. Ever since 1984, when both of them had been sent to cover the Democratic convention, in San Francisco, they'd been friends. He and his boyfriend, Walt, lived in our neighborhood, and the four of us got together when we could.

Just then, Nick's partner, Wendy, climbed out the other door. She was carrying a camera four times the size of Helen's, and almost as big as herself. Even someone as tall as Nicholas, at six feet, can get back problems carrying broadcast equipment, which is one of the reasons Helen changed to being an editor when she did.

Wendy waved and came around to our side. We knew her pretty well, too. Basically straight, she'd had one passionate affair with a woman, a few years before, on which Helen and I had advised her. But it ended up the same way her relationships with men had, with a kind of bitterness on both sides. A lot of straight women come to affairs with gay women, thinking the intimacy is going to be easier, and when it isn't, on top of everything else, they go back to men.

Having shot hours of the parade, Nick and Wendy were waiting for the crowd to clear, so they could drive the truck back uptown. The reporter they were working with, a woman the two of them called Queen Elizabeth because of her upright posture on camera, had just left to take the cassettes to the newsroom.

"She'll do the usual six o'clock package about drag queens and jockstraps," Wendy commented. The rest of us nodded.

"I edited the parade last year, you know," Helen said. "I put in shots of several wholesome-looking people, including a lot of interracial couples." She turned to Nick, who was white and whose boyfriend was African-American. "Then the producer saw it and he made me start over. Ultimately, they wanted something trashy...But what are you two working a weekend for anyway?" it occurred to Helen to ask. All three of them had the seniority to get Monday through Friday, day shift.

"Didn't I tell you?" Nick said. "We went back to weekends, until July, because I'm working on a documentary that I needed to shoot on two consecutive weekdays last month."

I thought it said something about what had happened to the networks that most people did their real work on the side.

"So what's it about, Nicky?" Helen asked.

"Siamese twins," he answered. That was probably the last subject either of us had expected.

"You should see the rushes," Wendy said. She handed Nick the camera. "They're the sweetest, most beautiful little girls."

"They share a stomach," Nicholas added, "which is where they're attached. They also share one heart and one digestive system. One of them eats and the other goes to the bathroom. They're four now," he said. Wendy opened the truck's back doors for him to put the camera inside.

"But how did you get onto Siamese twins?" I asked Nick.

"They're my cousin's daughters," he explained. "She lives in North Carolina with the girls and her husband."

"I want to see what you shot," Helen said.

"Well, I have a rough cut in my locker at the garage if you want to come up now," Nick told her. So we decided to go back with them to the station and watch it. But first we had to wait for the parade to end and the crowd to finish moving west in order to move the truck.

After we dropped it off at the company garage and picked up Nick's tapes, the four of us walked the half block to broadcast center. There was the usual bustle in the newsroom, particularly since it was so close to air, at six...anchors getting blow-dried, writers at computers, interns running tapes along the aisles. Though all the edit rooms surrounding the open sea of writers' and producers' desks were full, we found an empty one, around the corner, by the water fountain. It was Helen who slid back the glass door and seated herself at the editing console. It's union rules that nobody but an editor use the machines.

Nick handed her a cassette. The rest of us stood behind while she slid it into the playback slot and turned on the two televisions up above. It was crowded with four of us in a room the size of two closets, and the air a little close. But no one seemed to mind.

I'm not sure exactly what I was expecting. In a way, I hadn't pictured those two little girls at all. They were like a notion in my head...a set of words...still bodyless. It's one thing to grasp the *idea* of Siamese twins, but it's another thing entirely to imagine them, to see them in your mind's eye. Somehow the idea of a kind of double person was something I had to see for it to become real to me.

It turned out that Nicholas had set up the equipment the night before, on both shoots, and captured the two of them just waking from sleep. I say the two of them, but I wondered, while I was watching the girls come to consciousness, if in some ways it was more like being one person. The room was dimly lit by morning sun, and at first the whole scene seemed shadowy, as if to protect the girls from our vision, as they first began to reenter their joined bodies. This seemed right.

"Both nights, I slept in a sleeping bag in their room, on the floor," Nick told us. "The night before this shoot, I told them about a story we showed locally, this winter, though actually it was shot in the Midwest. It was about a Hershey's truck, carrying chocolate syrup, that got into an accident in Kansas and started leaking. All the syrup started pooling out over the street and onto the sidewalks, where it froze. The tape shows hundreds of children, down on their knees, banging with knives and forks." By this time, the natural sound had come up, and the girls were starting to talk to each other...saying things like what they might have for breakfast, first that they were too hot, then too cold, as they shifted the blankets. On the latter topic they were in complete agreement. As the sunlight intensified, you could see their faces more clearly. You could also see now that the room was inhabited by dozens of teddy bears and dolls, both on a bench at the foot of their bed and in a large open trunk near the door. The only stuffed animal with them in bed, on a pillow, was fantastically or not, a kangaroo. That is to say, two kangaroos...one in the other's pouch.

"That's Sarah," Nick said, pointing at the twin furthest from the camera. "And that's Annie on the right." The girls had begun giggling on the tape. "I wish we could have chocolate for breakfast, Uncle Nick," Annie called out. That was the only time they directly acknowledged his presence, but that interruption, oddly, threw you back into their world in a way that made it seem more authentic, less changed by the presence of observation.

The first edit was to the girls' discussion of getting up. It made me think how every simple decision most people make that includes some movement of their bodies was to these little girls a collaboration. I remembered Nick's comment that only one of them ate, while the other went to the bathroom. It seemed to me that they'd developed their own mutual ecology, something the rest of us could learn from.

After that, the girls did get up, which took some time, actually. They were wearing a garment I don't know what to call but that accommodated them both, like four-legged, four-armed pajamas, as together they inched along the sheets, then slipped over the side. And then the most interesting thing happened. Once on the floor, they walked...one going forward, the other back. It was like dancing. At the same time, it seemed like there wasn't enough room for the two of them in the space their union had provided, as they made their way to the bathroom.

"See how Annie holds her head up, while Sarah's droops down?" Nick pointed out. The two girls reminded me of swans, acutely aware of their necks. "Up until they were three," he said, "Sarah held hers up and Annie had the lower position. They're taking turns." This seemed to me the most touching thing I'd ever heard. I looked over and saw that Helen was crying.

"How long can you live like this?" Wendy asked.

"No one knows...but in their case, not that much longer probably," Nick said. Then he started crying quietly, too.

The tape cut to the two of them having breakfast in close-up. Wendy was right, they were beautiful little girls, with heart-shaped lips and long luxurious brown curls that seemed too mature for their tiny faces. The one who was eating, Sarah I think, continued to chew, while Annie started talking about the coming day at school...when they were going on a field trip to a farm.

"They go to school?" I said. Somehow I'd pictured them living exclusively in this intimacy we'd been privy to, though, of course, with their mother and father, who appeared later, but briefly, on the tape. The documentary was really about the girls and their relationship. I thought it was like some crazy arranged marriage, in which love is a necessity, though learned.

"Actually, they were worried about sending them, at first...because their environment had been so protected," Nick told us. "But Phyllis...that's my cousin, their mother... felt they deserved to know other people. So she went with them to school the first day, and sat with them and the rest of the kids, and explained their physical condition. She even took questions."

That's when I wondered how they'd first realized they weren't like everyone else. I pictured them discussing it with their mother, next each other, in their bed. But then I wondered what they'd known before language.

"They've never thought of themselves as freaks," Nicholas said, as the rough cut came to an end. But I thought that they probably had, because we all have.

"Do you think you'd ever march?" I asked Helen, later, when we were in a cab on our way to the Palladium.

"That's like asking if a woman could be elected President," she said. "So many conditions would have to change ahead of time, that you could never predict it. Either I'd have to be in a totally different career, or out at work, neither of which seems likely to me now."

Suddenly, the fact that I'd marched for peace, choice, disarmament, but never at Gay Pride upset me. Though I was out in my personal life, and also at the college where I taught, somehow being in that parade seemed unthinkable.

"I guess I'd be embarrassed," I admitted after a moment, "marching for sex."

"It isn't for sex, Chloe," Helen said. "We already have sex, unless I'm mistaken." I shook my head. "What people are out there for is everything else," she added, "like anti-discrimination laws and insurance that would cover your lover...fair reporting in the media." Once Helen had said it, this seemed exactly the point. It occurred to me that being a lesbian had landed me in far stranger places than the middle of Fifth Avenue.

We got out of the cab in front of the Palladium and went inside. The discotheque was filled with women, from the bar areas to the high-tech dance floor up into what had once been the seating of a concert hall. That was the only part left of the original interior besides the ceiling, reminiscent of Versailles. We looked for Rosalie and Alex everywhere, even in the women's room, and along the row of silver payphones. We went up to the balcony, where young girls, in pairs, were passionately kissing. They made me think of Monica and myself, once.

Downstairs again, Helen and I decided to dance. Though we were at least a decade older than most of the women there, I want to report that at forty there's still sex and romance. Pressed close to Helen's body, our breasts touching, I couldn't help but think of the twins. It was a position as perfect as could be imagined.

Actually, Helen was right. We never did run into Rosalie and Alex, who, we found out later, was so tired from marching while being six months pregnant that the two of them had gone home early. On the other hand, we'd run into practically everyone else we knew, from all corners of Helen's life and my own. I had a funny feeling, as we danced, the way you do sometimes, that our human sense of time, which pays itself out in days and years and decades, is an illusion. That, in reality, it all goes as fast as a single breath. I had a sudden sense of looking back on my whole life, the way you must when you're old, if you're lucky enough to become old. It's *then*, people say, that you understand it's nothing...a lifetime...just a wink in the eye of time. But actually, that night, it didn't seem to me looking back so much as looking into, the way a painting appears to change as you stand in front of it, while actually it's your mind that's in movement.

Suddenly, I pictured that parade coming down Fifth Avenue, and Rollerena like some fairy godmother of the world. I decided that if I, too, had the right to carry a magic wand, this is what I'd do: First, I'd make those twins live a long and happy life, though not necessarily apart. Then I'd make everyone come out at work. But I'd also take every respondent in a poll I read about, once, and change the 96 percent of them who'd voluntarily live next door to a black family to 100 percent, and the same with the 38 percent who wouldn't mind having gay neighbors. Then I'd make sure all the windows opened. Plus I'd spill a little chocolate every day. On top of that, I'd free Joanne Swift, and anybody else who needed it...which, as far as I was concerned, meant all of us.

Maybe that's why I thought next of my friend Harvey, who as a college student in the fifties had driven to another state to pick up men. Or Jill, who during that same era as a teacher in the New York public schools had to wear white gloves to class every day, by night risking arrest at a butch/femme club on Carmine Street. When you walked inside a gay bar, you could feel something like an undertow, and I don't think I was alone in considering it a point of honor just to take off my clothes and jump in. Because long before HIV, there was a sense both men and women had of being rushed by sex to oblivion...and, actually, for every person I know lost to AIDS, I can think of ten lost to drugs or alcohol or that masquerade that takes the place of selfhood when you're ashamed of who you are. I suppose that's why the Gay Pride parade means so much to us now.

"I think I'm going to march next year," I told Helen, as we left the club via Fourteenth Street. She stopped under the marquee and considered this.

"Well then, you better wear plenty of sunscreen," she said. It seemed a simple, addressable concern.

I moved in with Helen at the end of that month. The Arcturians did not take over the world.

Who & What Survives

The fashion show Julian had sold us tickets for was being held in an abandoned supermarket on Ludlow Street. As Helen and I rounded the corner, the building stood out among the tenements, its aluminum siding bleached the color of ice. Though the cooperative of arts organizations that rented it had been formed a few years before, that evening was the first time we'd been there.

Fashion sketches covered a brown paper liner that ran the length of the store's plate glass front. A hazy light emanated from the fixtures crowning the window. As we crossed the street, I thought about how strange it was to see a crowd, and a crowd like that, in front of a supermarket. Though most of them were older, like us, people who'd been around, there was the usual squadron of youth. Boys in porkpie hats and sculpted haircuts...dressed in black knickers and T-shirts, kimonos, constructed shirts. Girls wearing every conceivable article of clothing, from labcoats to leather jackets over ball gowns.

The formerly automatic *In* and *Out* doors were both open, with ticket sellers just inside. But no one seemed in any hurry to enter, and neither were Helen and I. It was one of those rare nights in July when all the humidity drops out of the air.

As it turned out, several of the designers Helen had worked with, when she was in the fashion industry, had donated their clothes to the evening. While we stood near the double doors, going over the names on a poster, headed *Over Our Shoulders: The '70s*, Helen marvelled that she recognized so many of them from years ago. Head designers of workmanly lines or assistants to the well-known, most maintained studios in Soho or the East Village, where customers could buy their originals. All made a living, though none had become famous. Of Helen's circle at the time, only DD had, which explained why her name topped the poster. That night, the model was going to walk a runway for the first time since her retirement at the end of the seventies.

"DD was one of the top ten fashion models in the U.S. and Britain, in 1972," Helen told me, after we'd moved up the sidewalk to look at the drawings on the runner. Everyone around us was talking.

"Did you know her, too?" I asked. Helen nodded.

"I met DD *before* she was famous...in 1969. You can't usually make friends with well-known people unless you are, too...because they think you want something from them." Helen mentioned the designer, like so many others now dead from AIDS, who had given her her own start as his assistant, while hiring DD to model his first collection that took off. "We knew each other during the two years both of us worked for him," Helen went on, "beginning when I was twenty. After the 1971 season, which made his name, and DD's, she signed contracts with Mary Quant then Courreges. I didn't see her a lot, though we kept in touch on and off until she moved back to London."

"Why didn't you see each other?" I wanted to know.

"Because our lives had become too different," Helen said.

"So how is it that a model like DD decides to come out of retirement for a twenty-five-dollar-a-ticket benefit in an old supermarket?" I asked next.

"Why not? These are the people DD started with...But she must have come mostly for *Alfie*," Helen said, using the designer's nickname. "I don't think DD ever would have had that kind of success without him," she continued. "Not that she wasn't talented...she was *very* talented. But DD was working as a showroom model at the time, and a lot of girls spend their careers right there. Actually, I think Alfie recognized something in her that even *she* didn't know about yet...

"Besides," Helen circled back to my question, "a model has her moment, then it's over. It's like being a dancer or an athlete...your body is both your opportunity and your limit. DD was lucky, actually, to be in the right place at the right time. She was British, she was nineteen, and her body was perfectly proportioned for miniskirts, and those dresses without waists. DD didn't have any hips at all." Helen cocked her head in remembering.

"You seem pretty familiar with her proportions," I said.

"I was a designer at the time," Helen reminded me. "Bodies become a kind of vocabulary for your *ideas*. Plus," she said, "though fashion is filled with gay men, most of the women are straight. I myself was, then, or thought I was. But you have to have a feeling for women to dress them," Helen admitted, "no matter who you sleep with.

"You see whole collections that are fueled by misogyny, both men's and women's," she went on. "But when I was designing for those few years in the early seventies, it was right when the women's movement had begun, and fashion reflected that. There was something joyous and liberating about the bold patterns and primary colors...for the designers as well as the women who wore them. No doubt, I was sublimating my homosexuality in my work," Helen said. "I was always drawing, or sewing something, in those days."

People were beginning to funnel through both doors now. It was ten to nine. But nothing in this city starts on time, and we stayed outside a little longer.

"So, what were you doing while DD was becoming so famous?" I asked Helen.

"Working...hanging out," she answered. "Going to clubs, openings, the movies. I shared an apartment on First Avenue, uptown, with a girl I'd met at a party. Her name was Sylvia. She got upset whenever a man slept over—I had a lot of one-night stands in those days—or if any of my friends ate her food, which they always did when we got stoned. She and I got along terribly," Helen said.

"Then why did you live with her?" I wondered aloud.

"Because she liked to go home to her parents' house in Queens every weekend, and I'd have the apartment to myself. Most of my friends at the time were the gay men I'd gone to design school with. We'd have these all-night parties, listening to Judy Garland records and sewing," Helen recounted. "On Tuesdays, the manager of Bendel's would buy what we'd made over the weekend. Customers' friends would show up at the store wanting to buy the same dress, but no one could remember, from one week to the next, what they'd made. Some of the really talented boys created look-alike Diors or elaborate party gowns from sample fabrics we'd find on trash days in the garment district. Women were getting hand-finished originals for fifty-five dollars...Sometimes I can't believe that was my life," Helen said. I knew what she meant.

"Sylvia got a wrong number in our apartment once," Helen recalled. "Well, not technically a wrong number...I'll explain that...but she ended up having a long conversation with this guy who called one night, who said he was a deejay and lived in New Jersey. She was so desperate for a date that when he asked her out she said yes, sight unseen."

"Today you wouldn't do that," I said. "You'd be afraid the guy would turn out to be a psychopath."

"Men weren't exactly reliable in 1971," Helen reminded me. "Charles Manson had recently masterminded the ritual murder of Sharon Tate and company...and a few years before, Richard Speck had trapped those nurses in Chicago and stabbed them one by one while the others listened outside the bedroom door...not to mention the Boston Strangler, who killed women who let him into their apartments, thinking he was a repairman. But you're right that once upon a time you didn't expect your average blind date to murder you."

"So what happened," I asked.

"Well, after they'd talked a while it came out that he knew Renee, this aging cabaret singer who'd originally held the lease to our apartment, which is why he had the number. Renee was a trooper...and glamorous, by our standards at the time, I think because she was French. So Sylvia figured the guy must be all right, maybe even interesting, and told him to meet her the next night at the apartment. But then she got cold feet and asked if I'd be there. I figured I had to say yes.

"I didn't think he could be that bad," Helen went on. "I agreed mostly to make Sylvia feel better. But when he got there, she immediately called me out of the bedroom, because she didn't want to be alone with him. He was incredibly strange, and he had painted-on sideburns."

"What do you mean, painted-on?" I asked. "Dyed?"

"He drew them in with Magic Marker," Helen said. We both started laughing. "They'd been planning to go to Chinatown for dinner, and Sylvia didn't know how to get out of it, so she invited me along. The deejay was pissed."

"Was he really a deejay?" I asked. Helen shrugged.

"He did have a case of 45s that he brought along with him...and, in all fairness, he had some great records. But you couldn't imagine anyone actually hiring this character."

"Weren't you humiliated to go out with him in public," I said, "with the sideburns?"

"Well, you have more tolerance for what's strange when you're young," Helen said. "Besides, there were a lot of weird people around then, so it wasn't so noticeable as it would be now. And I figured the Chinese would just chalk it up to crazy white people."

I started laughing again, and Helen joined me, in remembering. I thought about how funny life was then, and though it had to do with being young, it was also the spirit of the era.

"We got into his car downstairs," Helen went on. "It was a

Buick Skylark, with a huge front seat, and Sylvia sat pressed against the passenger door. He made a point of announcing to her that he wasn't going to pay for me, so she told him *she* was. I remember the guy asked if it was a double date. It was the only funny thing he said all evening."

"Right in front of you...how rude," I said.

"Rude was the least of it," Helen continued. "After we got to the restaurant, he and I had a huge argument about abortion, which was illegal at the time, even in New York. If you think I'm bad with men now," Helen said, "you should have seen me when I had more to do with them. Sylvia didn't speak at all. I think she was relieved. After that, he wanted to take the Holland Tunnel straight back to New Jersey. But I got him to drive us home by hinting we might ask him up to the apartment. He was that desperate."

"Everyone in this story sounds desperate except you," I remarked.

"Oh, I was just as desperate," Helen said. "But not for sex...that was easy enough to come by if you didn't insist on love, too. My problem was, my mother was dying, and I couldn't bear for her to leave me." Helen paused. "Sylvia moved back to her parents' house a few months later."

"Because she was traumatized by her date with the deejay?" I asked.

"I don't know," Helen answered. "But sometimes people just get ground to a halt in life. At a certain point, they can't go forward."

We stepped into the crowd that was streaming through the doors in earnest now. Once inside, we followed people around a partition at the back of the lobby to emerge behind some bleachers. You could hear a live band getting louder, as we walked up the narrow corridor. When we reached the front, a dozen musicians were fanned out behind the stage.

There must have been another entrance, because suddenly a crowd started pouring up the bleachers from the opposite side. As Helen and I climbed the center aisle, the floor surrounding the stage and runway grew choked with people. That's when we saw Miranda and Tanya T., about halfway up, waving from the middle of a bench. They'd saved us seats.

"I can't wait to see this show," Tanya said, leaning across Miranda's lap. It was the only time in the years I'd known her that she'd projected any hint of enthusiasm. Though the seventies wasn't her decade, the fact that the show was retro clearly excited her.

"The whole thing's like a time warp," Miranda commented. She pointed to the rows below, where several people were wearing fashions from twenty years ago. We picked out a Nehru jacket, four Beatle wigs on as many boys, a caftan made from a real flag. There were plenty of beads and tie-dyes, too. After that, Helen began quizzing Tanya about her fall collection, two samples of which she and Miranda were wearing that night. As usual, the dresses looked like thrift shop specials, Miranda's a sort of Tyrolian peasant jumper and Tanya's a cocoonlike shantung sheath.

A moment later, the lights blinked on and off. Then the music built to a finale. In the silence that followed, a man wearing a gray ponytail, and a black silk shirt and trousers, walked from the wings. Over the applause, Helen told me who he was. It turned out I owned a jacket he'd designed. Next, he pulled a sheet of paper from his pocket and began reading about the Gay Men's Health Crisis, in a monotone that would have been unthinkable in front of that audience only a few years before. I thought about how everything had changed in New York since AIDS. *I don't see what's so gay about it now*, a friend of mine's mother had put it quite succinctly.

The music started up as the speaker walked offstage, again to applause. The lights changed. That's when DD, who in retrospect looked exactly like you'd imagine, made her first entrance of the evening. If I say I responded to her right away, I don't know whether it was because of her history with Helen or the standing ovation she got, as people all around us jumped to their feet, shouting the two syllables of her name.

DD was dressed like a typical downtown fashion model, circa 1970. Wearing a kind of leather crown and an off-the-shoulder tunic with ankle boots, she looked like she was already living in the twenty-first century. It was funny how that image harked back, in some real sense, to the *past*. People believed in the efficacy of the future then.

"She's wearing only Alfie's designs," Helen said, when DD appeared a second time, in a geometric mini-dress that dropped like a small sail from her shoulders. "This was from the early seventies. There's something hopeful about that dress," Helen said, and it was true. After DD had made her way offstage again, a pair of twenty-year-olds, dressed in Marimekko jumpsuits, retraced her paces.

The evening continued. Helen and Tanya named the designers whose work they recognized, as well as made commentary on the collection DD wore in memory of their friend. Model after model traversed the runway, each outfit bringing back years it was both exhilarating and painful to recall.

"It's historic," Miranda said, "to see these clothes here tonight."

Time seemed to inflate, until finally the music swelled and DD appeared in Alfie's signature dress of the era. Even I recognized it. People rose, applauding, in the bleachers, before the rest of the models poured forth from the wings. After parading in concentric circles at the perimeter of the stage, they too began clapping, having turned to the celebrity in their midst. It was only then, as she stood surrounded by youthful bodies, that I actually registered how much older DD was. My mind did a double-take, the way it does when you see someone on the street who in passing reminds you of someone you knew. Only, after a moment, you realize that was what the person looked like *then*. And that years have passed in the meantime, aging everyone, including yourself.

Suddenly, sitting in those bleachers, I had a terrible yearning to be twenty again. For a moment I thought this had to do with the people and ideas I missed from when *I* was young.

But then I realized it wasn't so much about things that actually had happened, but about what might, the way at that age you have a whole life ahead of you in *imagination*.

You could feel the energy in the room as DD crossed the stage a final time, a phenomenon that went beyond the simple worship of beauty, or even fame. There was something about her bodily movements that looked less like training than a state of grace. It occurred to me that this was DD's talent.

The lights went bright, and the stage was empty. Helen started shaking her head, while Miranda kept sighing on the other side of me. Tanya just sat there, uncharacteristically quiet, until the aisles began to clear. After the band started up again, the four of us walked down to the reception.

We lost Miranda and Tanya almost right away in the crowd. People were packed shoulder-to-shoulder, and the areas around the refreshment tables at stage left and right were particularly dense. I was wondering if we'd run into anybody else we knew...like Victor and Ed Moss, or Teddy and Keith, all of whom had bought tickets that night at Miranda's. It was in turning to avoid someone that Helen didn't want to see that we ran smack into Julian, behind us. Helen and I congratulated him on organizing a wonderful evening, and he seemed exhilarated but grim, the emotion you saw so often in gay men. Then, in quick succession, we ran into first Victor, by himself...next, Tanya's assistant Roy...and finally DD.

The model remembered exactly who Helen was, and seemed happy to see her. After the two of them kissed and hugged, their talk and gestures remained animated, over the swell of the band. They reminisced about people and places, particularly during their time together with Alfie. Then, for the briefest moment, a looked passed over DD's face that I can describe only as a combination of rapture and despair. That's how I felt about the past myself.

Not too long after that, a pair of models, sleek as greyhounds, spirited her off. That's when Helen decided enough was enough, for one night, so we headed back alongside the bleachers for the exit. It was on the way out that we ran into Rosalie and Alex, coming through the door from the lobby. Because of her research, which overlapped work on the HIV virus, Alex was on the board of GMHC. Oddly, she and Rosalie appeared to be just arriving. It was nearly eleven-thirty.

"You two didn't get here now, did you?" I asked.

"I'm afraid so," said Alexandra, looking wistful. "We missed the whole show."

Helen and I were usually late ourselves, but not that late. It seemed out of character for doctors, particularly one who was seven months pregnant and often fell asleep now over dinner. Alexandra looked exactly as she had the last time we'd seen her, only as if her body were being viewed against a shifted horizon, enlarging it.

"We stayed through visiting hours at the hospital, then we took Margery out to eat," Rosalie explained. The music was still so loud behind us that I thought I hadn't heard her right.

"The hospital?" Helen repeated. That's when Rosalie's face changed, like a patch of ocean suddenly ruffled by wind.

"You don't know?" asked Alex. Helen and I shook our heads, and I started to get this queasy feeling, like I was adrift in that same ocean. "Burt was supposed to call you," she said. The last time we'd seen him had been at his mother's house in Westbeth, that terrible night with Ramon. Actually, I'd been afraid *he* might be the one in the hospital.

"Carol was admitted to Memorial Sloane-Kettering, yesterday, for surgery." Rosalie ended that particular mystery.

"What kind of cancer is it?" asked Helen.

"That's the unbelievable part..." Alex said. "Carol doesn't *have* cancer."

Rosalie interrupted her, "The whole thing was a mistake...someone read the ultrasound wrong. When she came out of the anaesthesia and the nurses told her, they all started crying...because that never happens...in that hospital hardly anybody ever gets off."

The four of us pondered this turn of events. Though it was just a mistaken diagnosis, it had more the quality of a miracle.

The next evening, after Helen got out of work, I met her in the lobby of Memorial Sloane-Kettering. I knew that hospital from before because of a friend of mine, who over the course of the last year of her life was admitted there seven times. The last time, Barbara's friends, most of whom didn't know each other, formed a healing circle in the lobby. I would have been embarrassed, standing there holding hands with twenty people in public, if I hadn't been so upset. She had leukemia, but it could have been anything toward the end...her eyes drawing strange arcs, her will in high gear, her body all swollen from the treatments. Though we were instructed to envision her recovery, I kept having this involuntary and repetitive thought, *Let Barbara go*. She was thirty-seven years old, a single mother with two kids.

Helen and I went over to the woman at Information then up in an elevator. All around us, people showed the strain of uncertainty in their faces. The oddest part of that evening was knowing that Carol was all right, at least for the foreseeable future. It's a feeling you seldom have.

We got off on six, and followed the signs that pointed us to Carol's room. It's true that hospitals declare night early, but it was also the atmosphere of a cancer floor, I think, that made that corridor so quiet. Inside the last room on the left, as we approached, we could see Carol propped up in bed, near the door. She looked wan and certainly tired, but peaceful as she sat reading a book, which I saw, when we stepped inside, was a travel guide to Italy. Marge was snoring in one of those cubist vinyl hospital chairs, pulled up to Carol's guard rail. In another bed, by the window...the sunset behind her a deep summer pink...was a girl in her early twenties, who looked up and smiled as we walked in the room. Her straight brown hair looked like a waterfall with bangs, her features pretty but too softly defined for my tastes.

"We're glad you're OK," I told Carol as we stopped at her bed. But I said it softly, because I was thinking about the roommate, who probably wasn't, as well as Margery being still asleep. Then I hugged Carol's head, from which she'd luckily just removed her magnifiers, because I was afraid of hurting her incision. Carol explained that she was fine, except for the pain from the surgery and a terrible case of indigestion, the reason she'd sought medical attention in the first place.

Margery woke up suddenly and denied that she'd been asleep. Actually, with two owlish circles under her eyes and a bone tiredness that showed in how she adjusted herself in the chair, she was the one who looked like she'd been through major surgery. On the other hand, Marge had lost a son in Vietnam, had one day abandoned a twenty-five-year marriage to live with another woman, then, at fifty, left the theater for direct-mail marketing. It took more than a false cancer diagnosis to scare *her*.

"Can you believe this?" Margery addressed Helen and me. We shook our heads.

"This is Deirdre," Carol rose, gingerly, on her elbows to introduce her roommate, "who's twenty-three and a waitress from Trenton, New Jersey. Deirdre rents a room, not far from Trenton State, and is considering starting college, part-time, in the fall."

Helen and I said hello. The girl seemed both too young and too unfortunate to be there by herself, like that.

"What courses do you think you might take?" I asked.

"I don't know," she answered.

This was a legitimate reply, under the circumstances. But I confess I wrote Deirdre off, then. I thought she was simple, and unsophisticated, which later turned out to be both right and wrong.

"I was just operated on for breast cancer," was the next sentence out of the girl's mouth. It sounded like she was rehearsing saying it. I didn't know what to answer. I just stood there, looking stricken, which was no help at all, and it seemed

Margery and Carol had pretty much exhausted their own resources, by then. But Helen, whose instinct for action in the face of all obstacles has buoyed me too when I most needed it, suggested we all write our congressmen and the AMA. For a moment, Deirdre looked purposeful, as if this act in itself would ensure her recovery.

Actually, this subject was a familiar one among our female friends, and it followed a familiar course. Carol brought up the fact that so many women we knew had put all their time and energy into AIDS activism in the last years, while more of us, by far, got breast cancer every year. Not to mention such other problems, endemic to women, as poverty and lack of access to safe affordable abortion, as well as widespread discrimination in housing, employment, and the legal system.

"Women are afraid to do anything for themselves. It makes them feel guilty," Margery complained. "All they know how to do is help everyone else." To the four of us, who of course excluded ourselves and a lot of other women we knew from such a gross generalization, this was a self-evident truth. But I could see Deirdre considering what Margery had said.

Meanwhile, out of the corner of her eye, Helen had been watching the TV that hung from the ceiling over Carol's bed. For her, television sets, with their continuous images and sometimes farfetched information, exerted the fascination, and fulfilled the function, of a crystal ball. Carol had the sound turned down on what appeared to be a talk show.

"Speaking of women, what's with her?" Helen said just then, pointing at the screen. We all looked up to see an ungainly female guest, sitting with her ankles crossed, in a tailored seersucker skirt suit. Towering over the male host, she looked like a cross between some Midwest businesswoman and a wrestler.

"Oh, I was watching this when you came in," Deirdre said, pointing at her own set, the twin to Carol's. "She used to be a man. Her name's Lucretia...*before* it was Luke."

"You'd have thought transsexuals would be old hat by

now," commented Margery, who, having lived sixty years and in New York, had seen everything.

"I guess they are," Deirdre answered, "because the topic isn't about being a transsexual really, but about how she became a feminist only three weeks after her operation." That's when I realized I might have underestimated Deirdre.

Helen walked over to Carol's TV and reached to turn up the volume. The program was one of those scandal magazines that come on, weeknights, at the hour when you used to get the network news. It was like coming in on the third act of an opera.

"Every time I call home and get my father, he just slams down the phone," Lucretia was saying. I liked her instantly, how forthright she was, and plucky. In her position, you'd better be. "For about six months, my mother wouldn't speak to me either," Lucretia explained. "But now when she picks up, we talk, and she says she's working on my father to renew our relationship."

"It's been five years," interjected the host. "Do you honestly think your father is going to come around to accepting you?"

"No," Lucretia gave him the short answer.

The interviewer continued asking Lucretia about friends' and family's reactions. Though I knew that was the point of the job, to extract personal information, I still couldn't get over the way he treated his guest...how he could be so ruthlessly curious about something so painful. But then I remembered that this was TV, which appears to be a record, a facsimile, of life, but isn't.

After that, Lucretia told the audience that she'd been an Eagle Scout, won a letter in riflery in high school, and in general had succeeded at her life as a man. When, a year before the operation, she announced her intention to have a sex change, which she did straightforwardly, as would be her way I was beginning to see, first her family disowned her, then her boss fired her, and after that Lucretia was dishonorably discharged from the army reserves. Most of her friends stopped calling her.

"As a man," Lucretia went on, "I had a lucrative career as a chemical engineer. My intellect was respected...I was very highly paid. But when I became a woman...at that point I was working freelance...suddenly people started second-guessing my judgments. Later, I couldn't get any work at all. I had to completely retrain in order to change careers. Now I'm a lawyer," Lucretia said. At this piece of information, we all looked at one another, incredulous. "*And* I'm a feminist. I represent women in sex discrimination and harassment cases, custody battles, divorce proceedings, etcetera." After that, Lucretia announced that she'd also become a lesbian. The fact that the host looked perplexed proved he didn't get anything about anything.

"She's impressive," Deirdre said, looking over in the direction of Carol's bed. Then she burst, loudly, into tears. It was Margery who, tired as she was, got out of her chair and walked over to Deirdre's bed. "I guess I'm just not brave in the face of adversity," the girl added, crying even harder as Marge began to stroke her forehead. Sobs racked her body, so deep that I was afraid she might physically hurt herself.

"Breaking down has nothing to do with being brave or not," Helen called over. I pictured Carol's nurses weeping in the recovery room.

Unlike in the movies, Deirdre did not look more beautiful for having cried. Her eyes puckered up, her skin got blotchy, her voice started squeaking as she spoke. For some reason, she launched into a monologue about breast reconstruction, going into considerable detail...about saline implants, ways to form a nipple, the pros and cons of silicone for long-term use. It's amazing what the mind can think about the body, while being a part of it.

Just then, Alex and Rosalie arrived, the former carrying a *Three Lives* shopping bag and the latter a bottle of Pepto-Bismal. Burt brought up the rear with two bunches of flowers.

This entrance with gifts had a sort of three-kings affect, the way certain stories get recreated all your life.

"Try this," Rosalie said. Carol unscrewed the cap on the bright pink liquid and drank, before picking up one of the half-dozen paperback mysteries Alex had spilled out onto the top sheet. Over by the window, Burt kissed his mother, then Deirdre, distributing the bouquets. The young patient called hello to the two doctors, by name; she'd obviously met them yesterday. Meanwhile, Helen got up and began arranging the flowers, as uncharacteristic an act on her part as could be imagined. I think she needed something to do.

"Do you think I'm going to make it?" Deirdre turned abruptly to Rosalie. Somehow Deirdre couldn't acknowledge that Alexandra was a doctor, too, seemingly because she was pregnant. You could see Alex trying her best not to get irritated.

"I don't know," Rosalie answered, after a moment, with the kind of thoughtful candor that is her trademark. "But there's better odds for breast cancer now," she added, "because of early detection and better treatment." You could see Deirdre concentrate on this piece of information...hold it up, look it over...her own kind of crystal ball.

"If I ever get out of here, I'm going to quit my waitress job and go back to college." Deirdre spoke loudly, in that same voice she'd used to announce her cancer. The words had a searing quality, as if burning oxygen from the air. "Maybe I'll even become a lawyer," she said. Deirdre paused for a moment from her vows. "I'm the only one in my family who ever reads a book"—she pointed at Carol's bed—"who likes to sing or dance. Even my boyfriend's just a zombie...he's the son of the family where I rent my room...how convenient for him." Deirdre shook her head. "If I live, I'm going to ditch them all," she added. "I want to live," the girl made her point more directly. All this time Marge had been stroking the bangs from Deirdre's forehead, while Helen kept playing with the flowers. The rest of us just listened, which was the point, it seemed to me.

Suddenly, a nurse stuck her head in the doorway and insisted that all but two of us leave. I realized then that Helen and I had already made up the maximum of two visitors per patient, which meant that Alex, Rosalie and Burt were technically not supposed to be there. Marge hardly considered herself a visitor, having taken up residence in the room three days straight from noon to midnight, which she started to explain. But the nurse turned out to be new to that floor, and young, and she wasn't about to bend any rules. At that moment, Deirdre produced her own solution, dramatically, like conjuring a rabbit.

"Two of them are with me," she said, triumphantly.

"I'm still counting six visitors here and only four allowed," the nurse continued her logic according to the new numbers. She was tough and sardonic, a combination I've always found hard to resist. I smiled at her. She smiled back, looking me up and down, then asked which two of us were leaving.

Because of their politics, Rosalie and Alex would never try to intimidate a nurse...not that this one was a likely candidate. On the other hand, you could tell they had no intention of leaving when they'd just got there. Burt, as usual, deferred to his mother, who first argued with then tried to charm the nurse into letting everyone stay. After that, both Carol and Deirdre complained...with equally poor results. Finally, Helen and I volunteered to go. It was fair, because, with the exception of Margery, we'd been there the longest.

Satisfied, the nurse brushed past me. Then Helen and I made the rounds of the room, kissing everyone good-bye, including Deirdre. That's when Carol announced, with some surprise, that the Pepto-Bismal had cured her. We all applauded, though Margery noted it might better have been prescribed earlier, before major unnecessary surgery had been performed.

"So much for modern medicine," Helen summed up. Working in the news, she'd become cynical about almost everything. But in this case, even Rosalie and Alex had to agree with her. Deirdre added that maybe she'd become a doctor instead of a lawyer, which caused both Rosalie and Alex to look pleased. But you knew it was unlikely her life would come to that, even if she survived...unless some miracle happened to Deirdre, too.

The sky was just darkening over York Avenue, the air quite warm though still without the usual stickiness. Helen remembered a Japanese restaurant in that neighborhood, on a cross street between First and Second, where we decided to go. It was a Thursday in July, and the Upper East Side was already deserted for the country.

Helen returned to the subject of Deirdre, wondering where she'd go to recuperate, at home with her parents or at her boyfriend's house in the rented room. It turned out that in Helen's childhood, her own family had taken in boarders. This was something I hadn't known about, the way, with even a longtime companion, the story of a life is inexhaustible.

"Well, at least you got to meet other people," I said. "Most families just wall themselves off, and then the world at large is a total surprise."

"That's true," Helen answered, "and I guess the extra money allowed my parents to do things we wouldn't have been able to do otherwise. Like eat and buy clothes," she joked.

"How much did the boarders pay?" I asked.

"I remember this woman Betty, whose rent was fourteen dollars a week. That was in the fifties," Helen told me. "Betty was a very unfortunate person, and older than any of the other boarders I can recall. She was in her late forties. Most of the rest of them were young Turkish women."

"Why Turkish?" I wanted to know. Helen raised her eyebrows.

"That's just the way it worked out. We were popular by word of mouth in that circle. But the real question remains how, in a country where women aren't even allowed to go to restaurants, those girls got out in the fifties and sixties to study in the U.S. They must have been geniuses," Helen said. "One of them, Matal, was a scientist, who was studying artificial fibers so that she could go back to Turkey and run a textile factory.

"They were awfully lonely, those Turkish girls," Helen went on. "They used to take me to the movies all the time. We'd see sexless comedies like *The Parent Trap*, with Hayley Mills, or else some Italian scorcher with Sophia Loren. Considering the two extremes, I don't know what they made of Western womanhood..."

By this time we were at Seventy-first Street and had already checked out the block between First and Second where Helen had thought the restaurant was, but wasn't. So we decided to try the next few blocks. Helen thought the restaurant might be on the right; definitely, it was down some stairs. We would have looked it up in a phonebook, or called information, more accurately, because there aren't any phonebooks on the street anymore...people destroy even the metal call boxes now. But she couldn't remember the name, either.

"Where did the boarders live?" I asked Helen.

"In the room upstairs next to mine," she replied. "When my grandparents from Russia were still alive, they had the two bedrooms upstairs as a suite, while my brother and I shared a room on the ground floor opposite my parents. Then, when I was still a little girl...my grandparents both died by the time I was five...I asked my mother if I could have one of the upstairs rooms. Eventually, they moved in a boarder up beside me. Years later, when I was in high school, we stopped taking boarders," Helen added. "Then my brother moved upstairs, too, and my father made the downstairs into a den."

"I guess that's why you're so good at living with me," I considered. "You've had lots of practice...with a wide variety of people." Helen nodded.

"And that wasn't limited to the boarders," she reminded me.

It turned out that the restaurant wasn't on either of those

blocks, so we tried the next one. We'd been snaking back and forth between First and Second avenues, like this, for half an hour. I think it was having been at the hospital and also the fact that it was summer that slowed us down to a more human tempo.

"Where was Betty from?" I returned to Helen's story. "Some other country, like Turkey?"

"No, Queens..." Helen answered. "Rego Park, to be exact, where she'd been living with her sister and her sister's husband. But the husband didn't like her, and she had to leave."

"That's pretty sad," I said.

"And it gets sadder," Helen told me. "It seems that her real mother had died when she was very young, and then her father and stepmother took care of her and her sister. The stepmother kept the two of them home all the time from school to do the housework, and was cruel to them."

"This sounds like the story of Cinderella," I said.

"Only nobody was Cinderella," Helen answered.

"How did you know all this?" I asked. "Did she tell you?"

"My mother told me," Helen said. "She was trying to explain to me what was wrong with Betty...what her problems were. Betty worked in this small department store...it had only one story, which was the type they had then...that was owned by the sister's husband on Union Turnpike."

"In fairness to the husband," I interrupted, "he *did* spend all day with her. It's a bit much to be asked to be with someone all day and all night, particularly if you don't like them. Was Betty likeable?" I asked Helen.

"No," she answered. "Betty didn't have any friends besides her sister...and because of the stepmother keeping her home all the time, she didn't have even a grade school education. Betty didn't really know anything."

"She didn't have any prospects," I repeated a phrase from my own youth.

"Every night," Helen continued, "Betty would practice typing and stenography. She had a manual typewriter set up on the bedside table in her room. I would hear her, through the wall, pounding away on the keys. Mostly, what she typed was business letters."

"How did you know that?" I asked again.

"She showed them to me," Helen said. "She typed them out of a book."

"You mean the two of you were intimate?"

"I was in school," Helen explained, "and I knew about writing letters. Plus, I think she was embarrassed to go to my parents, who were too tired at night to take an interest, anyway. Actually, I think she needed someone to talk to. So, no, we weren't intimate," Helen finally answered my question, "but we had a relationship."

"How old were you?" I asked, because I was starting to get suspicious.

"Eight," Helen answered.

"I can't believe you," I heard myself saying what I often did to Helen. "Not only do you remember everything from when you were eight, but you understood the world then, too. You gave advice. You had relationships...with people in their late forties. When I was eight, I was just a little girl."

"In some ways, I was always an adult," Helen mused. "I chose the furnishings for our house, and I also helped my parents pick out their clothes...remember I went into fashion design. My mother liked to take my brother and me to foreign films," she remembered, "because it was cheaper than going by herself and hiring a baby-sitter. So I spent most of the fifties and sixties in a movie theater, either with her or the Turkish girls. It gave me a sense of life. That's how I knew, even at age eight, that Betty didn't have one."

"Typing business letters," I said. "That's also like something out of a fairy tale...like spinning flax, every night, hoping it will turn into gold. And then, if the story had gone true to form, some boss would have hired Betty, then married her." But Helen emphatically shook her head.

"She also had me dictate letters so she could take steno. I

remember those letters vividly," Helen said. "They all sounded purposefully vague, as if, later, in a court of law, nothing would hold up. They were all written by men to men...men with names like Mr. Woods and Mr. Fleming. Here's an example." Helen stopped on the sidewalk and recited, "*Dear Mr. Woods: Thank you for your order of the twenty-fifth of November*. They always referred to some date in the past, as if it were real," she interjected before continuing. "*We will do everything possible to fill it by your aforementioned deadline and hope that we will retain you as a loyal customer*."

"That letter sounds like it's from another century now," I said. "The politeness, the enthusiasm, the unabashed willingness to please." Helen nodded.

"And after we used up all the ones from the book," she said, "Betty told me just to make them up. We used to sit in her room after dinner, and I'd dictate several letters a night. She wasn't bad at steno," Helen went on, "but I thought even then that it was unlikely she'd get a job. She wanted to be a secretary more than anything...that was her highest aspiration. But you have to remember that in those days all women could be was secretaries, so the competition must have been stiff. All the women who are executives now would have had to be secretaries then...or nothing."

"None of the secretaries can spell anymore," I said. "Plus the girls in the checkout at grocery stores don't say hello, and sometimes they don't even answer direct questions. Betty could have gotten a job today."

"If Betty were their age now, she'd be just like those girls," Helen corrected me. I thought this was probably true.

"What's wrong with them?" I wondered aloud.

"Well, for starters," Helen said, "they have no sense of the past or of community or being women." This made me think of Lucretia, who got the point in three weeks.

"So whatever happened to Betty?" I was pretty sure I didn't want to know the answer, but I had to ask, as just then we'd reached what Helen at last declared to be the restaurant. Its name was Yoshi Sushi, and the entrance *was* down a few steps but on the left. There were a handful of Japanese businessmen inside the vestibule, and the tables we could see were all full. So we came to a halt on the sidewalk.

"Well, she stayed with us for several months, without mishap," Helen answered my question, "and then one morning she came out of her room and accused my mother of sneaking into her closet and spilling coffee on her new winter coat. She said my mother was jealous of the coat."

"So Betty was nuts," I said. Helen gave me a look as if to say, With a life like that, who wouldn't be.

"My mother had to explain to me what *paranoid* meant," Helen continued. "When my brother and I were little, she would take psychology books home from the library and try to read them. My father used to make fun of her. He was against any kind of education because he never had one himself."

"Did it help you with your childhood problems?" I asked.

"Not at all," Helen answered. "But it was a way for my mother to show her love for us."

We swung through the revolving door and inside, where only the hostess was waiting now. After we walked to two seats at the sushi bar, greeted the chef, and sat down, Helen finished her saga.

"Anyway, my mother told Betty she had to leave. She was torn between feeling sorry for Betty and wanting to get her away from my brother and me. Plus she didn't need the aggravation. After that, we got the Turkish girls, which was better all around. They had simple problems...like culture shock and unwanted pregnancies." Helen laughed.

"You don't know whatever became of Betty, do you?" I asked. It was more an idle question than anything else, because I figured she didn't.

"If you can believe this," Helen replied, "the only time I ever saw her after that was fourteen years later. It was the day my mother died, when I was coming out of the hospital in Queens, and Betty was just climbing on a bus. She looked the same, only older. And I kept thinking, here's somebody who nobody loves and who doesn't love anybody, and she's alive. And there was my mother whom I loved very much and who loved me like life itself, who was dead. It didn't seem right."

"It isn't right," I said.

The next morning, it felt like my body was being pulled from the bottom of a lake with no surface. I knew I wasn't asleep any longer, but I couldn't wake up, either. I heard something like the old sound pattern on a TV.

"What's that?" I asked Helen, whose weight I could feel in the bed beside me. But by then I'd realized it was the clock radio. I reached to the windowsill and killed the new-music station. "Why didn't you just hit the snooze button?" I said.

"I forgot," Helen admitted. "I can't imagine why, but this morning I forgot there *was* a snooze button. I was afraid I'd oversleep if I turned it off." She rolled onto her back before continuing, "That's what they say happens with Alzheimer's. It's not about people forgetting where they put their eyeglasses... it's when they forget what eyeglasses *are*."

"What'll I do if you get Alzheimer's?" I asked.

"You'll take care of me," Helen replied quite seriously.

"OK," I agreed. "But I'll have to have a lover on the side."

"Just don't tell me about it," she said.

"If you can't remember what eyeglasses are, I doubt you'll remember about our relationship," I told Helen.

"Oh I'll remember," she said, running her hand across my hip. "You remember things like that in your body."

As farfetched as the rest of our conversation had been, I thought this was probably true, and I realized that if we separated because of Alzheimer's, or more likely for another reason, I would always remember her in my body, too. As we lay there, I recalled a friend of mine talking about leaving one lover for another and how it took years for the ghost, I'll say, of the one woman's body to be replaced by the other in her mind's eye. The ideal body, she called it, not in the sense of perfection but as the model or archetype...a mental imprint against the flesh.

"I had a dream last night," Helen said after that, "about my mother."

"I'm not surprised," I told her, thinking about the last few days.

"In the dream she wasn't dead after all, but had been kidnapped," Helen went on. "It was such a wonderful shock, that I thought she'd been dead all these years and suddenly there was a chance to have her back."

"I can imagine how wonderful that must have felt," I said.

"So I hired a private detective..."

"That's because Alex brought Carol those mystery novels in the hospital," I told her. But Helen waved, impatiently, in the air.

"I would have hired a detective anyway," she said, and the funny part was, she was right. In her dreams, Helen has the exact sensibility she does in life. Even the cast of characters is the same, and they're always in the same relationship to her. It's only reality that's different.

"So then what happened?" I asked.

"He couldn't find her," Helen answered. Then she started to cry, not loudly, the way people do to make themselves feel better, but the kind of crying that's about long-standing grievances. Life itself.

"Now that I think about it, I had the same dream about President Kennedy once, too," Helen added, "that he wasn't dead either."

"Did you hire a private detective to find him?" I asked, kissing her wet eyes.

"No," she said. "In my dream, he was just holding a press conference at the White House, as if he belonged there...as if he'd never been assassinated and everything had turned out *better* than all this." Helen waved her hand once more, then sank back into the bed.

"That's a sweet dream," I told Helen. Then the two of us got up and began the day.

Free Love

It turned out that the reason Victor had been by himself at the fashion show was because he and Ed had been having problems. In the month since then, those problems had escalated to the point they hardly spoke. Maybe it was ill-fated from the beginning, or maybe they couldn't get through to that stage where desire makes a sea change into love. And although Victor wasn't really so sick yet, you had to wonder if that had taken its toll, too. At any rate, our friend was suffering from what in hospital emergency rooms is called ROR...relationship on the rocks. They have a diagnosis but, as we all know, no cure.

In August, Helen and I spent a lot of time with Victor. We took him with us wherever we went, like a crime victim who's too traumatized to be alone. This was our own brand of first aid, surrounding him with the love of friends. But we were also hoping he'd meet someone new. That evening, we were taking him to Burt and Rob's for dinner. Carol and Margery would be there, too, along with several other people. We'd made plans to pick Victor up on our walk down to Soho.

"I doubt there'll be any eligible men tonight," I said, as Helen and I wound our way west, through the sidewalk book browsers and AA overflow, on St. Marks Place. "Everyone is either the wrong sex or sexual orientation, or too old, or attached, or all of the above."

"Well, you never know," Helen answered. "You meet people when you least expect it." I nodded. This had been true in our own case.

"Probably there won't be any reflexologists tonight," I said, with a certain disappointment. The last time we'd gone out together, someone had taken off Victor's sandals and tried to balance him through his feet.

"But I hear they've invited some *pagans*," Helen told me. I looked over to see if she was kidding, and she wasn't.

By this time we'd gotten to Broadway, and turned downtown. We began passing a string of boutiques for teenagers, whose tribal behavior outside made the sidewalk nearly impassable. The window dressings behind the plate glass fronts were constructions of clodhopper shoes and sacklike tunics over multicolored tights and torn bluejeans. The mannequins, and their real-life counterparts, looked like unisex Frankensteins...post-modern scarecrows...mutants from a nuclear leak.

We walked west on Houston, to where a dozen people were drinking coffee inside Angelika, waiting for the movies to start. Up ahead, a woman was exercising two little Jack Russells in the dog run. The sculpture in the driveway of one of the NYU highrises looked like some cross between a totem pole and a TV antenna, which seemed an accurate assessment of human knowledge. Things were more civilized here than in our neighborhood.

Victor was waiting for us, as promised, on the corner of Houston and Mercer. He looked deflated, the way people do when they've broken up with someone important. Our friend waved halfheartedly, before crossing the street. It was clear Victor no longer considered himself the host of life's party.

We walked down Mercer a block and a half to Burt and Rob's loft. As a working artist, Rob had rented it cheap, at the beginning of the eighties. While buildings all around theirs had been upgraded, assigned certificates of occupancy, in order to attract wealthy buyers, theirs was still illegal, and they were constantly in the process of being evicted, either by their landlord or by the city. There was something called air rights, which you had to own or rent access to in order remain a legal tenant. At the time, I'd thought, now this is what capitalism's come to...charging for air. But when Alice Eastman, a new tenant, moved into the apartment adjoining theirs, she sold Rob half her rights for a dollar.

Actually, the occasion tonight was in honor of her. That, and Carol's steady recovery from the surgery. Alice had become a friend of hers and Margery's in the few months since she'd lived there, being closer to their age than anyone else's. At seventy, she'd moved from a ten-room apartment on Fifth Avenue to a raw Mercer Street loft, which doubled as home and studio.

A widow who had married originally into the Kodak fortune, Alice Eastman was now free to pursue her art full time. Helen and I didn't know if this meant that Alice was an eccentric dilettante or if circumstances had diverted her attention from a true calling. But we'd find out soon enough. After dinner, she was going to model some jewelry and hats of her own creation. A jewelry designer himself, Rob hadn't seen this collection, but raved about her laser installations, on display in the loft.

We pressed the bell and after a minute heard the creaking of the ancient freight elevator, which the tenants in that building ran themselves. I was always worried that the tiny capsule wouldn't make it up to three, where Rob and Burt lived. As the door swung back, we glimpsed Rosalie and Alex inside, Alex so pregnant by now that the five of us could hardly fit in the elevator. It turned out that the two doctors had been on their way up when they'd heard the buzz, so they'd stopped and come back down again. To me, this was beyond the call of duty, even for those in a helping profession.

Suddenly, Rosalie pressed the lever at the back and the elevator lurched upward. I gripped Helen's arm.

"Steady pressure," Alex turned to Rosalie.

"I don't care if we drop," Victor said, taking some small pleasure in melodrama.

Upstairs, there were people I knew and people I didn't congregated near the dining table at the far end of the loft. Subdivided with curtains suspended from the ceiling at either end, for privacy, the one huge room was raw but majestic. Rows of open windows along opposite walls, facing the courtyard and an alley next door, let in a powerful cross breeze. It was almost like being outdoors, particularly since the loft was so sparsely furnished...with just the table and its straight chairs, and a sideboard next to two couches near the open kitchen.

As we got closer, Rob, taller than Burt and blond, made his way around the sideboard, wearing an apron printed with lobsters. Burt emerged from the kitchen, holding a serving plate, then began tap-dancing for Helen's and my amusement. Meanwhile, Margery and Carol stood nearby, talking to someone I figured had to be Alice Eastman. Tall and elegant-looking...what people used to call cosmopolitan...she wore her silver hair swept up into a French twist. But there was a bohemian air to her movements, too, as she turned to face a handsome Japanese man beside her. After we greeted our hosts, Margery introduced the five of us to Alice, then Kenji, who turned out to be Alice's assistant. He rented a room in her loft when he was in New York, Carol said, splitting the year between here and Tokyo.

The other people I didn't recognize turned out to be friends of Alice's...one woman a psychoanalyst who was visiting from San Francisco, another an anthropologist who lived uptown...both about our age. This left a heterosexual couple in their late forties, who had to be the pagans. Handing out business cards, the two of them introduced themselves as spiritual consultants. In the seventies, they'd probably been a witch and a warlock.

Rob and Burt finished setting out a buffet on the sideboard, then the rest of us helped ourselves to one of Burt's vegetarian quiches, assorted sashimi that Kenji and Alice had bought in a Japanese fish store near Bloomingdale's, and a cold turkey breast with vegetables made by Rob. The dinner was as eclectic as the company.

I ended up sitting beside one of the spiritual consultants, the man, with Rosalie on the other side, and the psychoanalyst from San Francisco and Kenji opposite. Helen was with Victor, down near the far end, beside Alice Eastman and Margery. Across from them, Gloria, the anthropologist, sat between Carol and Alex, who was next to April, the other consultant. Nearly everyone was already in heated discussion by the time Rob and Burt took the two stools at the head and foot of the table.

As might be expected, the conversation was interesting. Midway through eating, the warlock, whose name I finally latched onto as Otto, pulled a scrap of paper out of his pocket and began drawing what he called an energy diagram of the universe...a triangle...which included what he labelled a hook-up to God, the second position being humans, who in turn were grounded to the center of the earth. I should add that Otto was very stoned on something. April, who wasn't in such good shape herself, had walked down to our end of the table and now stood with her hands on her husband's shoulders. She added that *certainty* leads to *achievement* leads to *success*. I said I thought this proposition was probably true, but I'd always had trouble with the *certainty* part. Both Rosalie and the psychoanalyst, whose name was Judith, smiled.

Meanwhile, the rest of the table was listening intently to Gloria, whose specialty turned out to be cross-cultural sex differences. Every now and then, Helen would yell some fascinating fact she was hearing down to our end of the table. I remember two that stood out: first, that natural selection favored women, which was the only good news I'd ever heard about being female, and second, that men and women were two entirely different species, something many of us had suspected. That's when the analyst mentioned that a friend of hers, a psychobiologist, had done a study that documented thirty-six separate sexes along a continuum from female to male. Alex nodded, and actually, it didn't seem so farfetched, when you considered the range of people's sexuality.

After that, their end of the table branched off into a discussion of *mating*, when Gloria said that most people marry someone who lives within thirty miles of them. Helen glanced at me, then Victor, implying we'd been exactly right to drag him all over the metropolitan area. Meanwhile, our group had gotten onto the topic of who's sane and who isn't, which always comes up around shrinks.

"I knew a boy in high school who was a brilliant cartoonist," Burt was saying from the foot of the table. "He was voted most likely to succeed for the yearbook. Then, the summer after graduation, he took a sketching trip through Switzerland, where he got interested in levitation. Eventually, he gave up drawing for that discipline, which he practiced every day."

"Did he ever get off the ground?" Kenji asked. This was one of the few times I'd heard this phrase meant literally. Burt shrugged.

"People can, you know," Otto leaned over to tell me. "I saw it several times in India." Then he announced to the company at large, "I knew a young man who was incurably ill...so depressed he couldn't even leave the house...until, in desperation, he tried to blow his brains out. Well, it turned out he shot off only a small portion of his brain, though by chance, the correct one. After that, he stopped being depressed and led a normal life."

"It's possible," said Rosalie, who was the only one of us who knew anything about brain function.

"A sort of do-it-yourself lobotomy," Burt commented. People laughed.

"There's a therapy in Japan," Kenji mentioned next, "where you lie in a room, with sensory deprivation, for a week, and think about all the nice things your parents ever did for you. Then you get up, and you feel better."

"I sincerely doubt that," I said. Anyone in analysis would have reacted this way. But it's no way to talk to the Japanese, who are the soul of politeness.

"I suppose it might work in some cases," Judith assumed her best therapeutic neutrality. "But how much people recover and why is often a mystery. A friend of mine had a patient," she added, "a schizophrenic...who got cured then took a seat on the Stock Market. Occasionally, he'd have a slip and think the FBI was after him, but over a decade, he made millions." People nodded...not that any of us could really grasp either reality.

That's when I told what I thought was also a significant story about the human mind...about the time, years ago, that Helen saw Lucien Freud, a painter and grandson of Sigmund, on "The Tonight Show." The minute he walked out onstage, the television audience started laughing. Helen said he didn't seem surprised as he went to sit down. When the then host Jack Parr asked Lucien Freud if this happened to him often he didn't answer, but just stared straight ahead, stone-faced, while the audience shrieked with laughter. Jack Parr became furious, trying to get them to stop. He turned on the house lights and even lay down on the stage. But nothing worked until, ten minutes later, having not said one word, Lucien Freud got up and walked off again. Then the show continued.

"I can think of only one thing I ever witnessed that compares with that in...*mysteriousness*," Rosalie said. She gestured to Judith. "Once when I was in San Francisco at a psychiatric conference, I was borrowing a friend's office to prepare a response to a panel. Suddenly there was a terrible rumbling and swaying...the office was on the sixth floor...and you knew right away it was an earthquake. The building was full of private practices, and when I ran out into the hall, in a panic, I saw in almost every doorway a psychiatrist and patient holding each other. That's the safest place...in a doorway. Then the earthquake stopped and slowly the pairs untangled, going back into the offices and shutting the doors."

No one responded to this verbally…it would have been like trying to explain a joke. Then Burt began clearing the table.

After dinner, everyone got up to see Alice Eastman's work. It turned out that Helen and I hadn't really understood the geography of the two lofts. Alice had bought hers actually at a separate address from Rob's, just behind on Greene Street. Though technically in the same building, the Greene Street lofts were condominiums and had a separate entrance with a new elevator. Because the original lofts had been immense, originally running as factory floor-throughs, there was still a door between Rob's kitchen and Alice's studio, which they explained was never locked. So much for the theory that people in New York don't know their neighbors.

As we filed through the door, the experience smacked of through-the-looking-glass, as if a whole other existence were in progress on the Greene Street side, and actually, this turned out to be true. Boxlike installations on lucite bases were scattered throughout the maybe three-thousand-square-foot space. They looked like little altars, each one lighted from above. A dozen folding chairs had been set up not far from a picture window facing downtown, where a great deal of the city is in the sky.

A minute or two later, Alice Eastman disappeared into a kind of long closet or storage area, separated from where we sat by a wall of muslin suspended from two poles. It reminded me of early Cristo or a maze. This corridoring could be seen on several axes, crisscrossing that part of the space, making rooms out of air. The only sheetrocked, floor-to-ceiling walls had been built at either end of the loft, where *shoji* screens were used instead of doors. One led to Alice's apartment, and the other to Kenji's room, Rob said, after all of us had sat down on the assembled chairs. That's when the Kodak heiress walked out from behind the roofless tent, modelling her first hat.

Pillbox-shaped, the hat was fashioned out of pipecleaners. Two bracelets, also from pipecleaners, wove up her arms like long-sleeved lace gloves. Though it might sound silly, these objects had a sculptural effect that was breathtaking. Beyond the picture window, the twin towers of the World Trade Center looked very close, like on certain nights when the moon gets magnified. After that, Alice Eastman walked back and forth from the corridor of cloth, modelling several other hats and accessories...belts, necklaces, a tiara, even a kind of evening jacket like ornamental armor. The way Alice moved, with both ease and purpose, reminded me of a woman showing her nakedness...that was how much art meant to her. Part of the brilliance of these pieces was that they were made from a material that was simple, useful, and cheap.

Frankly, it wasn't for doctors...a seventy-year-old woman parading around with pipecleaners on her head. You could see both Rosalie and Alex getting impatient as they sat there, particularly Alex, who the more pregnant she'd become, the more short-tempered. No one was right or wrong...it's just that artists and doctors pay a different kind of attention. I thought about this difference when next, Kenji demonstrated the laser art, because you can also do surgery with that light. They looked like colorful models of something I couldn't quite put my finger on, something basic, until Alice Eastman explained that all her projects were inspired by DNA. That's also when Alex started taking a new interest.

Meanwhile, April and Otto looked nonplussed. As pagans, and stoned ones at that, I believe they thought Alice had tapped into the fourth dimension of the universe. This reminded me of the role art must have played in pre-scientific cultures, when metaphor was the only form of knowledge. Marge and Carol, as artists themselves and longtime devotees of the avant garde, had taken a keen interest in everything that transpired that evening, though you could see Carol tiring over its course. In the front row, Judith, the analyst, and Gloria, the anthropologist, were involved in intense discussion...probably about sex.

Then people got up and looked at the boxes on which Alice

had collaborated with Kenji. That's the kind of artist and woman she was...someone who called work with her paid assistant collaborations. These pieces were contemplative in nature, reflective, in contrast to the implied activity of the laser beams, and even the virtuosity of the pipe cleaners. They had such titles as "The Moon Reflected at Night on Water," and "The Ordinary Is Not...Is Not," the latter sounding more like Dada or Gertrude Stein than anything Eastern. The materials in these pieces were found objects...twigs, leather pockets, mirrors, eggs.

At a quick glance, the boxes appeared similar, but the longer you looked, the more your eye got attuned to the subtlety of the variations. Looking at them, like most real art, was an acquired vision. Each work demanded attention, time, and reference to a larger aesthetic context. There was one titled "The 44 Strokes of Melancholy," which Kenji started explaining to those of us standing nearby. Victor looked stricken as he stared at the little box.

"In Japan now," Kenji said, "we have a generation gap that's the result of simplifying our written language, particularly with the use of computers. *Konjee*," he pronounced, "is a pictorial system of characters, some of which explain very complicated abstract ideas. For example, *melancholy*, which is composed of forty-four brush strokes, is only four keys on a computer. Mine is the last generation really literate in *konjee*.

"It's a problem of philosophy," Kenji continued. "Take our character for *newness*. Literally, it means 'cut the branch'...the sappy flesh represents the new."

"It's poetry," Alice Eastman said, as if there were no higher compliment. Then she moved off to illuminate another piece.

Around midnight, Carol and Margery, along with several of the others, exited via Rob and Burt's loft, where they'd left their things. Soon after, Kenji took Helen, Victor and me down in the Greene Street elevator. The three of us waved good-bye to him, then stood for a moment on the sidewalk.

Up the block, loading docks jutted from the shadows, all dark wood and metal like the hulls of freighters.

"Do you think Alice Eastman is sleeping with Kenji?" I asked Helen and Victor as we walked along. We were making for the cross street, which was Broome, in order to stroll up West Broadway. "I mean he's right there in her house, half the year...and they work that closely, and they're both so soulful...so what if Alice is twice his age."

"Stranger things have happened," Helen replied, "and I wouldn't put it past Alice, or him. You know how artists are..."

"On the other hand, they may be of no interest to each anywhere along the spectrum of the thirty-six sexes," Victor added. "It could be just an inexpensive way for Kenji to live in New York."

Another artist I met, this musician Winston Wong, had had a similar arrangement with my friend Philip, who also had a loft, back when I was breaking up with Sydney and staying there for a while. But Winston didn't even rent a room, just part of the floor. Each night, after getting home late from a gig, he unfurled his sleeping bag in the entryway, behind a staircase. Philip said this routine never varied, including Winston's awakening at noon, then heating up either mock chicken stew or vegetarian chili that he bought in cases from the health food store. Winston Wong never stayed anywhere for the night and never went out to lunch. He'd needed someone to hold him, I thought now...like I had myself at that time...in a doorway or, better, in a bed.

Though I didn't tell Victor, my ace in the hole for him was Bob Remick. Unconventional yet reliable, single but a father-to-be...he seemed the perfect set of contradictions to intrigue someone of Victor's sensibility. Bob was also a relative, in the sense of friendship, through both Rosalie and Alex, and Sandy's dance troupe. It was Sandy who inadvertently made their meeting possible, by inviting Helen and me to a political fundraiser, at his boyfriend Ricardo's, of all places, in Spanish Harlem, one hot day near the end of August. Several of the Dancing Fools would be there.

The suggested contribution, collected by Ricardo at his apartment door that afternoon, on the third floor of a walk-up on Second Avenue and 106th Street, was five dollars. At first this seemed low, especially since it included lunch. But as we entered the room, which was a sit-in kitchen that opened into a small living room, and saw the handful of people sealing envelopes and making posters, I realized that we'd been invited as volunteers.

A somewhat short and square-built man in a simple white shirt and navy trousers came forward to greet us from the living room. This was Carlos Martinez, the candidate, who was running for City Council in Ricardo's district. He was personable, and forthright, as he shook hands with Victor and Helen and me, and I thought took to campaigning like a natural.

"This is my *goombah*," said Ricardo, kissing Carlos on the lips. In New York, all ethnic language is interchangeable. "There should have been a lot more people here," he went on. "But it's so hot, everyone went to the beach." This was the most words we'd ever heard Ricardo speak, and actually, the first time we'd seen him in sunlight. Sandy walked up and put his arm around the younger man, also the first gesture of intimacy I'd witnessed between them. Their relationship seemed to have deepened since the incident with the water.

"What's your campaign slogan?" Victor asked Carlos.

"Cure our crises," Ricardo interjected. It wasn't a great slogan, but the idea was correct. Then Carlos introduced us to Albert, his campaign manager, who we found out later was also his lover. Carlos was a cop, of all things, and Albert, a social worker.

I looked at the assembled company for Bob Remick, and couldn't find him. But the older woman with whom he'd danced at the Food Fund Benefit was at the stovetop, the only surface free of campaign material, stuffing ingredients into tacos. Two men, dressed as pirates, in leather boots and headscarves despite the heat, were handing out beer and soft drinks from a cooler under the table, where they sat licking envelopes. Sandy introduced them as Herbert and Maurice, recyclers who subcontracted for the Parks Department, their territory being the whole of Central Park.

After we got some food, Sandy took us into the bedroom, which turned out to be the largest room in the apartment. Here a half-dozen more people, including Bob Remick, were sitting on the floor and bed. They were making a banner for Carlos and Albert to hang from the window of campaign headquarters, also their apartment, on the eighteenth floor of a nearby highrise, where you'd be able to see it, heading north on the FDR. That's when I noticed Bob's other dance partner, on the floor across from him, stitching at the large rectangle of felt. I hadn't recognized her, at first, because you don't necessarily think of a blind person as sewing.

I was hoping to persuade Victor to help with the banner, particularly since the bedroom had the only air-conditioner. But he said he preferred to lick envelopes and left to return to the kitchen. Helen was ecstatic, and immediately sat down with the sewers. She said later that the blind girl, Elena, had the smallest stitches. Meanwhile, I joined the group on the bed, who were cutting out letters from orange canvas. Ricardo gave me scissors and several squares with chalk-lined C's. An aging gay man named Howard, wielding the stick of chalk, was our art director.

That's when Ricardo began talking about his recent projects in the neighborhood and at large: visits to the local community board to get a sign on 107th Street changed from No Parking to alternate-side rules, joining the citizens' crime patrol, writing talk shows to protest the treatment of gays and lesbians. On welfare, Ricardo felt he should work for the money, but at a job that was significant to him. Sandy said that, running a dance company, he was in so much debt that he might soon need assistance himself.

I think it was the mention of welfare and debts that got us onto the topic of bill collection. Howard, who for years had owned a travel agency, told about getting a business loan once, which he'd paid off only to find out later that it was mistakenly sold to some collection agency. It all started with a phone call from Western Union, telling him to call an unidentified local number. But when he did and asked the secretary who answered what company she worked for, she told him to hold. Then, when she came back, he asked what her name was, and she put him on hold again. Finally she got back on the line and told Howard they were coming to collect his furniture.

"Can you imagine?" Howard said, from where he sat next to me, tracing letters. "When I finally got the full story out of her, I told her I'd paid that loan. And you know what she answered? 'That's what they all say.' It went on for months like that, even after I sent them the paperwork."

"You should have called your congressman or Betty Furness," Helen said.

"I had better things to do in those days," Howard replied somewhat grandly.

Just then, Victor walked in, with the pirates and the historian of modern dance. He seemed liberated in a way I hadn't seen him in some time, or maybe he was just drunk. The four of them sat down to help, but all they really did was talk. Helen said the afternoon reminded her of art school, where everyone told stories and sewed.

The word that came to mind was *paradox*, when Sandy continued, with a story about his uncle who, by law, had to have the asbestos removed from a boiler in a building he'd bought. The cost was steep, at $45,000, to remove the waste and haul it to West Virginia. But he was willing to pay until he found out he was just renting space at the other end, because he actually still owned the asbestos, and would for three generations. So that his children, then his grandchildren, even their children, would inherit it, remaining responsible for relocation if and when the West Virginians didn't want it anymore.

"And who in their right mind will want it as time goes on?" Sandy said. "It's like playing that game where everybody dances around a bunch of chairs and when the music stops, you sit down, only they're always one short."

"Musical chairs," Bob Remick said, shaking his head. I think it was clear to everyone, by then, that things had gone completely haywire in our country and beyond.

That's when Carlos said that we were a culture in crisis, victims of both *technologism*, with its runaway philosophies of computers, genetic engineering, and military conquest even in space, and also *urbanism*, with its crime, pornography, and drugs. His own platform called for treating the city as cosmos or Global Village, stressing ecological activism, and experimentalism, anti-authoritarian values and neighborhood priorities...in hopes of reestablishing a society that *served* people. The alternatives were corruption, dehumanization, and thought control, he said, which he needn't have added had become a trend in recent years.

"A friend of mine from when I used to live in New Jersey has a son with cerebral palsy," Albert added. "From birth, Billy needed these special exercises with his arms and legs, which she did. But then he became too big for her to be able to do them anymore...she didn't have the muscle strength. So I suggested she take him over to the reform school I used to work at and see if some of the kids there would do it. At first there were no volunteers, just draftees...but then they grew to love Billy and had to start a rotation, so many of them wanted to exercise him. Three years later, when his mother moved away, they actually asked for another boy."

"Like a pet...or their own child," someone said.

"They'd grown connected to the human race," Carlos clarified. "In *my* New York, everyone will feel needed, because they are." This was true enough. "There will be jobs for all who want them"—he nodded toward Ricardo—"except for unrehabilitated criminals." That was the only time, all afternoon, that Carlos had sounded remotely like a cop.

I reflected that though our candidate had real solutions to a number of the city's problems, he would never in a million years be elected. Not with his people-first politics and the fact that he was an out gay man in a Latino community. On top of everything, he was running against a minister. I wondered why he'd become a candidate when the odds were so clearly stacked against him, so I asked.

"I'm not really sure," Carlos answered. "Among my people, you always come up through grass roots, because we don't have any other kind of power. I suppose it's an old-fashioned strategy, starting small and trying to grow larger in name-recognition and support, but word-of-mouth was the only way I could think of to proceed. This race is just my beginning," Carlos explained. "I intend to keep running till I win."

By this time the banner was done, thanks to Helen, who had single-handedly sewn on thirty-seven letters out of forty-eight. We invited whoever was left in the other rooms to come look at it, though by this time it was around four, and still incredibly hot, so that a lot of people had already left. After everyone was assembled, Sandy and Ricardo lifted the banner from the floor. *Vote for Carlos Martinez for City Council* loomed larger above the slogan *Cure Our Crises*, which, I had to admit, had grown on me. This act had the drama of raising a sail. Then Elena went up and read it with her fingers. She looked like someone scaling a mountain, which is what Carlos himself had set out to do.

We all filed into the kitchen for a toast. Nearly everyone and everything you could think of got mentioned...including Victor's homage to Baudelaire, about decadence and spirituality...as well as the future, Spaceship Earth, lithium. People toasted Gandhi...Rosa Parks...Anne Frank. Cold fusion, feminism, the Goodyear blimp. Redwoods. Haiku. Moving pictures. Footnotes. Skin grafts. Microchips. Dreams.

Afterwards, the candidate went into, then came out, of the

bathroom—dressed for duty. To his dark regulation pants and shoes, he'd added the shirt and hat, plus accessories. Victor, who was sitting at the kitchen table, was particularly taken with his gun and handcuffs, and you could see Albert looking proud from across the room. Even Bob Remick and Sandy seemed attracted to the badge and the authority, though before they'd been quite happy sewing. This was the root, if I may say so, of all our crises.

Of the men present, only Ricardo and the pirates seemed unmoved. Also Howard, who had started dancing to the radio with Bob Remick's octogenarian partner.

"I'm a pacifist," Ricardo informed Helen and me, before nodding at Herbert and Maurice. "And they're against recycling people before they're old." I could see why Sandy was with him.

Then some of the others began to dance...for the collective it was like a busman's holiday. I was reminded of Emma Goldman, who insisted on dancing at her revolution.

"Any prospects?" I asked our victim of heartbreak on the way downstairs, shortly after that.

"No...no chemistry," Victor said, "cxccpt with that uniform. I sort of liked Herbert," he added, "but *you* tell *me*, would a pirate who collects cans fit my lifestyle?"

"Well, what about...Bob Remick?" I came right out with it.

"I hate overachievers," he commented, and I realized I should have known. Why else would a Ph.D. in history from the University of Chicago have chosen a career writing articles on hemlines and Caesar salads? "You know," Victor went on, "lovers come and go. But friends are the primary people in my life, from day to day and year to year. I sometimes think I'm not cut out for romance..." he added.

"No one is," I told Victor, as we stepped out into the hot street, full of people in tanktops. But I thought he might be right about himself, that friends, not lovers, were his true source of tenderness.

We hailed a cab at the corner, then drove straight down Second Avenue, with all the windows open. Victor sat in the middle.

"I don't know, Ed Moss just had that *je ne sais quoi*," he mused. "And that's something you can't manufacture...either it's there for you or it isn't."

"But then you have to figure out how to *be* with that person"—Helen nodded in my direction—"how to give and accept love."

"Well, what *is* that state?" Victor said. "I don't think I've ever gotten near it with a lover...not even Ed."

"It's like watching the moon reflected at night on water," Helen told him. What she meant was, you can't explain it.

While the two of them continued talking, I remembered walking up to someone I'd never seen before, in a restaurant, once, and asking if she'd like to join me for lunch, which she did, moving her plate to my table. She gave the most beautiful précis of the ingredients in the chef's salad without even pausing for explanations, such as who I was, or why I'd approached her, or anything of the sort, and offered no information about herself, such as she was supposed to meet someone else who didn't come or always ate lunch there by herself or even her name. We spoke almost exclusively about the food...nevertheless this was one of the most erotic conversations of my life. I ate everything with my hands, mostly off her plate, and she ate from mine. After lunch, we parted ways. She wore a wedding ring, and I think it was just one of those crazy things, as if suddenly you had lived two hours out of time.

Desire is like that; it has nothing to do with anything, but is like some lighted circle of the mind into which you step with another person, leaving the rest of life behind. Years ago, I knew a woman much older than myself who made my hands shake every time my body came within feet of hers, though she was overweight by then, and losing her looks. Attraction is irrational.

"You know," Helen was telling Victor, as we passed the construction on Twenty-third Street, "this conversation reminds me of when I was thirteen and stayed up all night reading *Summerhill*. Its radical values had completely changed me, and I wanted my mother to know. That morning, at breakfast, I told her I believed in free love."

"So how did your mother react?" Victor asked.

"She said, 'Nothing's free,'" Helen told him. We continued the ride in silence.

"Will you be all right?" I asked Victor, as the cab stopped at Thirteenth Street.

"Yes...in several years," he said, looking through the open door. This would have been funny if it hadn't been true. Or if we thought he would have all those years.

Helen and I walked the half block home, then climbed the steps of our building. Recently, they'd painted the vestibule robin's egg blue, so that you had the impression of being in Miami, or some other resort town. The fantasy of Florida faded as we approached our triple-locked door at the back, though I knew it was bad now in the cities there, too.

Inside the air-conditioning was on, and both Helen and I followed the hall directly to the living room, where it was coolest. We sat here, on a couch, amidst the stacks of magazines and newspapers that Helen always swore she was going to get through, but never did. The more she read, the more came in. Shelves on two walls were overstuffed with CDs, videotapes, and books on all subjects, the overflow in piles on the rug. I reflected that on a single helix of DNA, there was more information than we could ever fit into that one apartment. The same was true of our minds.

That's when the phone rang. It was Victor.

"Guess who?" he said.

"Shirley MacLaine?" I asked.

"No, but close. Dalai Lama here." This was the most lighthearted Victor had sounded in weeks.

"Hello, Dalai," I said. This was our running gag. "What's up?"

"Believe it or not, Alice's assistant, Kenji, just called," Victor announced. "He wants me to go to some galleries with him tomorrow."

I repeated this news to Helen, who, beside me, was clipping magazines. She didn't seem the slightest bit surprised. And, really, in a world where people make art from pipecleaners, and cure themselves by trying to blow their brains out...not to mention the unlikeliness of love...what's there ever to be surprised about?

"I hope you're going," I said into the phone.

"Yes," Victor answered. "I have no more illusions about love," he explained himself, "but I'm hoping for safe cross-cultural sex."

"You never know," I told him.

After we hung up, I thought about meeting Helen. It was at the first session of an adult-education course I taught on contemporary women playwrights. When she asked me if I wanted to go out for a coffee afterwards, I said yes, but only for coffee, as if I were actually replying to the other, unstated question would I go home with her...meaning no, because I didn't have the heart for it after all that had happened with Sydney. But I did go back to her apartment and had spent every night with her since then, starting over when, like Victor, I had every intention not to.

Why? You can't explain it any better than the reason people laughed at Lucien Freud or wish to hold their analysts in a doorway. It was something about her face in profile and how she said my name when she spoke to me, how my body felt in proximity to hers at a table in the crowded Cafe Dante. It was like falling in an earthquake, or being chased by the FBI.

That's why, when people are young, and haven't lived enough yet, they think they'd trade everything for a single person or one hope. But later, it's the fullness of life that's so thrilling. You think in *konjee* where before you had a keyboard.

Then you get tired of musical chairs, and there's something you want to add to desire...to do with longevity and dailyness...when the conversation expands well beyond the two of you, to your place in the world, such as it is...in Soho or Spanish Harlem...rich or poor.

I thought about how much happens in a single day, sometimes an afternoon. Maybe it was the people we'd met at Ricardo's...so various and particular...that suddenly made me see no one way of living as primary, from which the rest of us were variations or aberrations...but as if experience were a kind of kaleidoscope, with everybody just a hair's turn away from the next person, and on and on. But sometimes, for a moment, the kaleidoscope stops turning, and you can identify everything and everyone with clarity, for once. Like one of Alice Eastman's holograms.

Around Labor Day, Alex's baby was born. In October, Rodger died in his sleep.

This first edition of
Our History in New York
is published by
Global City Press,
New York City

It is designed by
Charles Nix

The text type is Transitonal 521
from Bitstream
after W.A. Dwiggins' Electra

Production was managed by
Burton Shulman

The printing is by
Offset Paperback Mfrs., Inc.
Dallas, Pennsylvania